What Happened to the Deer?

Grace + Gebriella,

Have fun reading This
book full of fun + adventure

Best wishes

Mary Ellen Ereston

Other Books by Dr. Mary Ellen Erickson

Grandma Mary & Bonbon Series: *First Day of School*
A children's picture book that teaches character building traits
and emphasizes rules and work ethics.

Grandma Mary & Bonbon Series: *Snowstorm*
A children's picture book that teaches character building traits
and emphasizes attitude, feelings, and cooperation

Common Sense Caregiving
A non-fiction book based on research
that stresses the positive side of elder caregiving.

Otis
Historical fiction about growing up in the 1950s.
This novel includes romance, mystery,
and some complicated family relationships.

Geezettes
The adventures of seven retired women.
This novel includes humor, romance,
and the importance of friendship.

Look for other *Peanut Butter Club Mysteries*
in the future.

WHAT HAPPENED TO THE DEER?

Peanut Butter Club Mysteries

Book One

Mary Ellen Erickson, PhD

iUniverse, Inc
New York Lincoln Shanghai

What Happened to the Deer?
Peanut Butter Club Mysteries

iUniverse books may be ordered through booksellers or by contacting:

iUniverse
2021 Pine Lake Road, Suite 100
Lincoln, NE 68512
www.iuniverse.com
1-800-Authors (1-800-288-4677)

Because of the dynamic nature of the Internet, any Web addresses
or links contained in this book may have changed
since publication and may no longer be valid.

This is a work of fiction. All of the characters, names, incidents, organizations,
and dialogue in this novel are either the products of the author's imagination
or are used fictitiously.

ISBN: 978-0-595-42799-4 (pbk)
ISBN: 978-0-595-68396-3 (cloth)
ISBN: 978-0-595-87136-0 (ebk)

Printed in the United States of America

Contents

CHAPTER 1

▼

GUESS WHO'S COMING TO VISIT?

Deer on the prairie

"Says here in the *Gazette* that they found another bunch of deer carcasses down by the James River last Saturday."

Joshua Philip Haskell was reading from the local paper.

"How many is a bunch?" his wife of forty years asked with skepticism while she stirred the scrambled eggs in her old, black skillet.

"Doesn't say."

"Well, you know the *Gazette*. They tend to exaggerate. Not much excitement in this small community, so when something different does happen, they blow it all out of proportion."

"Now, Abby, you know if it's in the *Gazette*, it's got to be true," Josh teased.

"Humph!" was Grandma Abby's final word on the subject as she finished preparing breakfast. "Put that paper down, and eat your breakfast before it gets cold," she instructed her husband, placing the plateful of food in front of him.

After filling her own plate and setting it on the table, Abby sat down and continued the conversation.

"Old Ulla needs to be milked right away this morning. I need some milk to bake that cake I'm bringing to the church potluck supper tonight."

Josh had a mouthful of food, so he nodded his head and continued to chew. The couple sat silently and ate their breakfast as they had done hundreds of times over the years.

Josh was a diversified farmer who lived northeast of Aberdeen, South Dakota, on the same small farm his grandfather had homesteaded over a hundred years ago. His good wife, Abigail April, a former country schoolteacher, had been his helpmate since they had married in 1964. She could be a bit cantankerous at times, but she was an honest, hardworking woman; he loved her dearly.

They had moved to the family farm shortly after their marriage, and Josh's parents had moved into Golva, the nearest small town. Josh's father had helped with the farming until he'd passed away fifteen years ago. Now Josh was retired.

Since their only son, Mark, had left the farm to pursue a degree in ophthalmology, Josh had no one to inherit the farm. Neither of his grandsons seemed interested. They were both too young to know what they wanted to do when they grew up. Maybe this summer he would show them that farm life could be fun and rewarding.

A smile crossed Josh's face as he thought about his grandsons. Dennis, the older, was high spirited and could be a handful but was also bright and curious. Josh liked that in kids—the livelier the better.

Tyler, Josh's younger grandson, was as cute as a bug's ear with his reddish brown hair and freckles. His mother, Sylvia, had spoiled him; at age seven he still acted like a baby.

Well, we'll change that this summer, Josh thought.

Josh's mind wandered back to when he was a young boy of seven. He remembered doing farm chores, riding horses, driving the old tractor, and herding cows.

Josh's thoughts were interrupted by his wife's voice.

"When you're done eating, will you please go milk Ulla, so I can bake my cake?" Abby said with a touch of urgency in her voice.

"I'm on my way, Abby—don't fret. You'll have your milk within the hour."

Josh finished the last bite of his food and got up to leave the house, grabbing his straw hat as he walked out the door.

✳   ✳   ✳   ✳

Abby had worked herself into a frenzy over the past week, worrying about her grandchildren's two-month visit. Abby's son, Mark, and daughter, Sylvia, had asked her and Josh to watch the children while they were on a humanitarian project in Central America.

Abby felt it was her religious duty to help with such an important mission. Since her daughter, Sylvia, was a nurse and her son, Mark, was an eye doctor, they were qualified to take used eyeglasses to the needy people in Central America and also perform eye surgery on those who couldn't otherwise afford to the surgery.

Her son-in-law, Thomas, was an optometrist and would help with the eye exams, while her daughter-in-law, Heather, a business woman, would be doing the paperwork.

Abby put her old straw hat on automatically and headed out to the garden. Her mind was preoccupied with thoughts about her four city-raised grandchildren and how she would manage everything for the next two months.

*   *   *   *

The garden was growing nicely. It had been an early spring, and everything had come up quickly. The rain three days ago had helped move the growth along. Josh had fertilized the garden this spring with some old cow manure that had been turning to compost the past twenty years. Unfortunately, along with the plants, the weeds were also growing quickly.

Abby grabbed her hoe, which was leaning against the garden fence, and started hoeing her onions, lettuce, and radishes. The onions and radishes were ready to eat, and the lettuce would be ready soon. She hoed furiously as she sang "Amazing Grace" with gusto.

When she got to the end of the radish patch, she spotted a baby cottontail under the raspberry bushes. He had been frightened by Abby's hoeing and singing.

Cottontail in raspberry bush

"Poor little guy, you're trembling," Abby said with sympathy. "Did you lose your mama?" she asked the brownish gray bunny as she picked him up. He fought for a moment and then became quiet as she restrained him in her arms.

"Well, I don't want you eating my lettuce, so I'll have to ask Josh to put you out in the woods. Maybe you'll find your mama there."

Abby went to the garden shed, put the bunny in a brown cardboard box, and added some straw. Then she went back to the radish patch and picked the biggest radishes she could find. She twisted the green tops off and threw them on her compost pile in the corner of the garden and started for the house. There was a cake to bake.

✳   ✳   ✳   ✳

When Abby entered the kitchen, she saw Josh sitting and reading the paper again. The milk was sitting on the table in an old, stainless-steel pail.

"Got another chore for you after you finish the paper," Abby told her husband. "I caught a bunny in the garden. I need him put a long ways from here so he doesn't eat my lettuce."

"Okey-dokey," Josh replied automatically as he continued reading his paper.

Abby put the milk that she wasn't using for her cake away in the refrigerator and got out her other cake fixings. She needed to finish the cake by noon so she could frost it and take it to the country church they belonged to. The church family had suppers once a month for anyone who wanted to attend the Wednesday Evening Songfests. Tonight it was her turn to help serve, so they had to be there early to get set up—Josh could help with that.

As she got up to get out her hand mixer to beat the cake ingredients, the phone rang. Josh answered.

"Hello."

Elmer, on the other end of the line, wanted to know if Josh had heard about the deer shootings.

"Sure have," Josh said. "Read it in the *Gazette*."

"What do you think about that?"

"Animals are always dying one way or another. I hate to see them shot for no good reason," Josh said thoughtfully. Then he added, "Probably some of them folks camped down by the river last week that done it."

"Those folks were some of our local Indians," Elmer began to explain. "It couldn't have been them. Native Americans don't hunt off the reservations. The deer they kill on the reservations, they eat. They wouldn't just leave dead deer lying around to rot in the sun."

"Never thought of that," Josh said. "Guess you ought to know the Indian ways." Elmer was a quarter Sioux.

"Yup," Elmer answered. "I'd say it was some city kids out for a fun time, thinking it was cool to shoot something. City kids sometimes don't have much respect for country creatures."

"You may be right, Elmer."

There was a long silence. Elmer spoke first.

"What are you and Abby up to?"

"Abby's busy baking a cake for the church supper tonight, then tomorrow we drive to Aberdeen to pick up the four grandchildren, who will be staying with us for two months. Abby is all riled up about that."

"Humph," Abby snorted in the background as she continued mixing her cake.

Josh laughed at his wife's irritation, and then added, "We're looking forward to having the little whippersnappers here this summer. Should keep us both hopping."

"Well, I'll send my grandchildren, Randy and Missy, over to play with them. How old are your grandchildren?"

"Let me see." Josh racked his brain and then looked at Abby for help. "I think Audrey's about twelve …"

Abby nodded.

"Tyler is six …"

"No, seven," Abby cut in.

"Seven," Josh continued, "Those two are Sylvia and Tom's kids. Then there are the twins, Dennis and Jennifer." He paused and looked at Abby.

"Ten," Abby called from across the kitchen. "They'll be eleven in about a month."

"They're ten," Josh said over the phone.

"That will work fine," Elmer said. "My grandchildren are ten and eleven. Not too many kids out here in the country for them to play with anymore. Do you mind if I bring them over after your grandchildren get settled in?"

"No, I'm sure Abby won't mind. It would be good to have the city kids meet some country kids. They might all learn something."

Abby was shaking her head and frowning at Josh inviting Elmer's grandchildren for a visit.

"I have to go," Josh said. Then he added as an afterthought, "See you at the church supper tonight, if you've got a mind to sing and eat."

"I'll see what Emma has in mind for tonight. We might just do that."

"Okay. Good-bye."

When Josh hung up the phone, Abby said, "That Randy Cavett is a regular outlaw, Josh. I don't know if I want him here leading our grandchildren astray."

"Now, Abby, don't worry. I think our grandchildren might lead the Cavetts astray. You know that Denny and Jenny can get into more trouble—in a short time—than you can shake a stick at. Those twins will be the death of their parents yet."

"I guess we'll just have to whip the whole bunch of them into shape this summer," Grandma Abby said with determination in her voice.

"I guess we will," Grandpa Josh replied, then turned his head so Abby couldn't see the grin breaking out on his face.

"I'll take care of that rascal rabbit," he teased as he left the house.

Abby shook her head slowly and thought, *I'll not only have four grandchildren and two neighbor kids to straighten up the next two months, I'll also have that fun-loving husband of mine to keep an eye on. You never know what he'll think up next.*

CHAPTER 2

▼

A LONG BUS RIDE

The bus trip from Sioux Falls to Aberdeen took over four hours, with the different stops along the way. Audrey Abigail Thomsen, the oldest, was in charge of the small flock of children.

At twelve years of age, Audrey was almost grown up—at least in her mind. The other children saw her as bossy, pushy, and no fun at all. Audrey took every challenge that was given her with extreme seriousness.

"You're in charge of this group," her mother, Sylvia, had announced as they said their good-byes before getting on the bus. "You'll see to it that everyone gets to Grandma and Grandpa's place safe and sound. The rest of you will listen to Audrey, or there will be a price to pay when you get back."

"I'll do my best," Audrey replied in her most grown-up voice, as her mother gave her a kiss on her cheek and then hugged and kissed Ty. Audrey had felt like crying, but she tried to be brave. She would miss her parents and friends.

Audrey took her cute, seven-year-old brother Ty's hand and walked up the bus steps. She paused halfway up the steps and called bossily to her cousins, "You two better get up here before you get left."

Denny and Jenny, the blond twin tornadoes, followed reluctantly. They didn't see why Audrey was in charge when they were only two years younger. They looked at each other and knew instinctively that they would give Audrey a bad time the next two months. Because they were twins and had been very close all their lives, they could read each other's minds. What mischief one didn't think of, the other one did.

Although the twins looked alike—tall, thin, and blond—their personalities were somewhat different. Denny was easygoing and wanted to please people. Jenny was more demanding and liked to complain about everything. Denny usually had a positive attitude about situations in life, while Jenny took a more negative view.

Audrey took a seat next to the window. The sun shone on her straight, shoulder-length, auburn hair. Audrey was big and strong for her age. If those twins didn't listen to her, she'd show her two skinny cousins her latest karate moves. Audrey had taken karate at the Y last year and was pretty good at it.

Ty took the seat next to his sister, because he needed her for protection. Denny and Jenny would pick on him at times, and Audrey always stuck up for him. Audrey spoiled Ty as much as his parents did.

Denny took out his Game Boy, and Jenny got out her CD player and headphones the minute they were seated. They would endure the ride by ignoring it.

"Will you play cards with me, Audrey?" Ty asked after the bus began moving.

"Sure, got a deck?"

Ty nodded. "Cool."

Ty got his card deck out of his backpack and mixed the cards. "Let's play Crazy Eight," he said.

Audrey put her small, carry-on suitcase on the seat between them, and Ty dealt. The game continued until the bus stopped at Brookings.

Denny and Jenny emerged from their technology comas and looked out of the windows.

"Why are we stopping?" Jenny asked.

"We're at Brookings," Denny replied.

"Oh. Let's get off and get a snack. Mom gave us some money."

"Okay," Denny answered and got out of his seat, followed by Jenny.

When Audrey heard the twins get up, she turned around and asked, "Where are you two going?"

"None of your bee's wax." Jenny shot back.

As the twins started down the isle, the bus driver saw them in his rearview mirror and announced over his speaker, "Stay in your seats. We're loading some passengers, and then we'll be going."

Audrey didn't say a word as they got back into their seats, but she gave them an *I-told-you-so* smirk.

Jenny stuck her tongue out at Audrey, put on her headphone, popped in her newest CD by Fallout Boy, and started lip-syncing along with the music.

Denny picked up his Game Boy and continue playing his latest game as the bus pulled out of the station to continue the journey.

*   *   *   *

The bus driver, a tall, stout man with a mustache, had been told by Audrey's dad to keep and eye on the children. When they arrived in Watertown he came to the back of the bus and told the children they could take a potty break at the station. The children knew instinctively, from the tone of the driver's voice, that this was the type of man they should listen to.

The children got off the bus and went to the bathroom. The bus driver watched the children like a hawk to make sure they wouldn't delay his bus.

After Watertown, the children got bored and began complaining and picking on one another.

"I want to go home," Ty whined as tears welled up in his eyes. Ty had never been separated from his parents for a long period of time.

Audrey tried comforting him.

"Don't be sad. We'll have fun at Grandma and Grandpa's farm. Just wait and see," she said.

Audrey knew how Ty felt. She remembered her first summer at Girl's Scout camp and how homesick she had gotten.

Ty buried his face in his hands and began sobbing.

Audrey took him in her arms and tried to console him, to no avail.

Denny heard Ty and peeked around the back of the seat. "What's the matter, baby?" he asked.

"Ty is a crybaby, Ty is a crybaby," Denny chanted.

Ty buried his face in Audrey's shoulder and quit crying. He didn't want to be called a crybaby, especially by Denny, who was kind of his hero. He liked to tag along with Denny when the older boy would let him. In Ty's mind, Denny and his friends were cool.

"What's going on?" Jenny asked as she took off her headphones.

"Ty is crying," Denny said.

"So, what's new?" Jenny said in a sarcastic tone of voice. After pausing a moment, she added, "I hate leaving my friends for the summer. This trip will be a real drag!"

Denny agreed. "Yeah, I know. We'll have to make the most of it. Maybe we'll meet some cool kids we can hang out with." He looked hopeful.

"There are no kids on Grandma and Grandpa's farm, and the farm is a million miles from anything," Jenny exaggerated in a negative tone of voice.

"Not a million. It's got a cool creek nearby and some awesome pets. Remember the cats and old Laddie?"

"That old dog stinks!" Jenny said.

"That's because he is an outside dog. Grandpa never washes him."

"Pee-hew!" Jenny frowned and held her nose.

Denny defended old Laddie.

"Well, he's a nice dog, and he knows tricks, and he used to be able to herd sheep," Denny said.

"Grandpa hasn't had sheep for years," Jenny said sarcastically.

"I know. Maybe Laddie misses the sheep."

"What a stupid thing to say," Jenny said with disgust, then put her headphones back on and drifted off into Fallout Boy land.

*   *   *   *

When the bus pulled into Aberdeen, it was almost noon. Ty was sleeping on Audrey's lap. The twins had also fallen asleep, because they had gotten up so early that morning to get ready to catch the bus.

"Wake up, everyone," Audrey said loudly. "Grandma and Grandpa are watching at the gate for us … see." She pointed out the window.

Denny and Jenny stood up and looked out the bus window, trying to spy the elder Haskells.

"Here we go," Denny complained, "to live in Neverland."

"Yeah," Jenny whined, "there's never anything to do. What a drag!"

"I want to go home," Ty whimpered like a small, wounded animal.

"For Pete's sake, all of you shut up and be good!" Audrey shouted in dismay above the noise of the passengers disembarking. "You want to disappoint Grandma and Grandpa? It isn't their fault we've been abandoned."

The other children snapped to attention as Audrey herded them off the bus.

*   *   *   *

"There they are." Grandma Abby pointed as the children descended the bus steps.

"They look so sad," she said. Grandma's heart melted, thinking of the children and how they must feel, being away from home for two months. She vowed right then and there to make their summer a fun one as well as a learning experience they would never forget.

"They'll be fine, Abby," Grandpa Josh assured her. "Let's go and welcome them."

Children standing beside the bus

The children were standing in front of the bus waiting for their luggage as the grandparents approached them with open arms and big smiles. There were hugs and kisses for all. Grandpa picked little Ty up and tossed him into the air, then held him tight.

"My you've grown, little feller. Bet you're ready to ride old Bessie by yourself. Are you?"

Ty had forgotten about Grandpa's riding pony, Bessie, so when he heard her name, a big smile broke out on his face.

"Can I, Grandpa, can I?"

"Sure thing Ty, as soon as we get home. Old Bessie likes little whippersnappers like you."

Ty hung on to Grandpa's neck when he tried to put the boy down, so Grandpa held him while Grandma and the other kids gathered up the luggage and headed for the car. Grandma was talking a mile a minute, trying to assure the grandchildren that they would have lots of fun this summer.

CHAPTER 3

▼

OH NO, NOT RADISHES!

"Since it's lunchtime, should we stop at McDonald's on the way out of town for something to eat?" Grandma asked the children.

"Yeah!" the children shouted in unison, as Grandpa covered his ears.

"Hold on there, kids. Not so loud. I've got on my hearing aid, and I think you just broke my eardrum."

"Sorry, Grandpa," Audrey apologized, looking very distressed.

"It's all right this once, but see to it that it doesn't happen again," Grandpa said sternly. Then he started the car, backed up, and left the parking lot.

As they drove down the street, Grandma looked into the rearview mirror and noticed how anxious the children looked as they sat quietly in a row.

"It's okay, sweeties," she said, turning around in her seat. "Grandpa likes to jerk your chain once in a while."

"What's 'jerk your chain'?" asked Denny.

"It means to tease you. You'll have to get used to it; he does that a lot."

Grandpa grinned. "Sure do, so look out."

The children all laughed, and the tension was broken. Maybe Grandpa wasn't as stern as they had envisioned him to be.

*   *   *   *

Lunch at McDonald's was a success. The children had eaten at McDonald's many times, so they knew just what to order. Denny and Jenny got the chicken nuggets Happy Meal, because they liked the toys inside the bag. Ty got French fries and a milk shake. He didn't like the Happy Meal toys, because they always broke when he tried to play with them.

Audrey ordered a fish sandwich with nothing on it and a caramel sundae. She had studied good eating habits in her health class last year and knew that fish was good for a person's diet. She didn't think that a sundae was too bad, because it contained milk.

Grandma raised her eyebrows at the orders but said nothing. This group seemed to be allergic to red meat and vegetables. However, she did insist they have a carton of milk each instead of a soda—there was just so much junk food she would tolerate.

*   *   *   *

"When are we getting there?" Ty asked after about fifteen minutes on the road. "I want to ride Bessie."

"Soon, child, soon," Grandpa assured him. "We've got about fifteen miles of gravel left, and then we'll be home. Do you remember what the farm looks like?" he asked the children.

"I do," said Jenny. "There's a big red barn, a white house, a small creek with a bridge, and a swing in the big tree in back of the house."

"Good description," Grandpa praised her. "Now, Denny, do you remember anything else?"

"Yes, there's a garden shed, a Quonset shed for machinery, and an old dog called Laddie."

"Very good," Grandpa said. "How about you, Audrey?"

"I remember the milk stalls in the barn, the chicken-wire fence around the garden, and the grandfather clock on the mantle that rang every fifteen minutes, so I couldn't sleep."

Grandma joined the discussion.

"Those are very good details," she said. "Now, Ty, what do you remember?"

"I remember the cookie jar in the kitchen, the kitties in the barn, and riding Bessie," little Ty spoke up boldly.

Everyone laughed, including Grandpa, who was trying to concentrate on his driving.

"Very good for all of you," Grandma complimented the children. "Let's play I Remember. We'll take turns, and when it's your turn, you can say one thing you remember. The next person has to say the same things the person before said, and then add one thing of his own. The last person will have to remember all six things that were said. We'll add on until there are too many things to remember. The person who remembers the most things will win the game. Okay?"

The children nodded their heads in agreement.

"You go first, Ty," Grandma suggested.

Ty grinned from ear to ear. "I remember the kitties in the barn."

Audrey went next, remembering the kitties and the big oak table in the kitchen. Denny added old Laddie, and Jenny remembered the swing. Grandma and Grandpa joined in the fun, and before they had completed the game twice, Audrey glanced out the window and announced, "There it is—there's the farm."

The Haskell farm

"You're right," Grandpa said as he turned the car off the gravel road, went over the bridge, and drove up in front of the house.

✳   ✳   ✳   ✳

The car was soon unloaded, and the luggage was put into the two bedrooms upstairs. One room was for the two girls, and the other room was for the two boys.

The girls' room had been Sylvia's room when she lived on the farm. The curtains were white with pink roses—they matched the bedspread. The furniture was white, and the carpet was a harvest gold.

The boys' room had been Mark's room when he was on the farm. The curtains had pictures of all types of sporting equipment on them. There was no bedspread; it had been torn years ago. The bedcover was a warm blue blanket. The furniture was a sturdy brown maple that was built to take a lot of abuse. The floor was the original hardwood that had been put into the house when it was first built in 1910.

"Do I have to stay with this crybaby?" Denny complained.

"You're both boys, there's one room, and I guess that's the way it will be," Grandma said. "Besides, Denny, this will give you a chance to learn to be a big brother. It will teach you responsibility."

Ty looked sad, and Denny looked mad.

Ignoring the reactions of her grandsons, Grandma said, "Now, unpack your things and put them away. After you're settled, we'll do some fun things."

The children came downstairs when they had finished their chores and gathered in the large country kitchen where the patterned linoleum on the floor showed years of wear. The kitchen cabinets were made of solid oak, as was the large, sturdy kitchen table that had six chairs sitting around it. The kitchen was warm and inviting.

Grandpa decided that he would take the children out to the barn to look for kittens.

The group was crossing the yard when a white car turned off the road and came over the bridge.

"That looks like Sheriff Whippert's car. I wonder what he's up to," Grandpa said to no one in particular.

"A sheriff?" Ty looked fearful. "Will he arrest someone?"

"No, Ty. He's probably just stopping in to visit," Grandpa assured him.

When the car pulled up closer to the group, a chubby sheriff with double chins rolled down his window.

"Morning, Josh. Got yourself some grandchildren to take care of?" the sheriff asked with a big grin on his face that made his eyes close into little slits.

"Yup. They'll be here for two months. Should be able to get some work out of these whippersnappers in two months—don't you think?"

"Sure do. Let me know if they're lazy pups, and I'll see what I can do about it."

Ty's eyes opened wide with worry. He was wondering if rural sheriffs put kids in jail if they didn't do their chores.

Sheriff Whippert changed the subject. "I'm investigating the deer killings down by the river. Do you know anything about that, Josh?'

"No, can't say that I do. I'll keep an eye out if I see anything."

"Good. I'd appreciate all the help I can get."

Sheriff Whippert smiled. "I'll be moseying along—got lots of ground to cover today," he said.

"Have a good day." Grandpa smiled back at the sheriff, then turned to the children. "Say good-bye to Sheriff Whippert," he instructed.

"Good-bye, Sheriff Whippert," they all said in unison.

"Good-bye, kids. Be good."

With that said, the sheriff drove off.

The first to speak was Audrey. With concern in her voice, she asked, "Grandpa, why are they shooting deer?"

"I don't know, honey. Some people are just plain mean, I guess," Grandpa answered.

Little Ty began tearing up as he asked, "Are they killing Bambi's mommy?"

Jenny reprimanded Ty.

"Bambi doesn't live here, stupid. That's just a story," she told him.

"That's enough, Jenny," Grandpa said, giving her a stern look. "Ty doesn't understand the difference between what is real and what is made up. Come on, let's find the kittens."

The children raced to the barn, with Grandpa following at his usual slow pace.

*   *   *   *

"Look at those beautiful little fur balls," Audrey purred as she picked up a white kitten with black spots.

Jenny picked up a kitten and said, "I like this gold-striped one. I think he will grow up to be the biggest. He's already the biggest one here."

"How do you know it's a he?" Denny asked.

"I don't. I just thought it might be, because it's bigger than the others."

Ty sat down in the middle of the hay where the kittens were resting and started to play with the four that were left. There was an all-white kitten, an all-black kitten, a calico kitten, and a black and white, tiger striped kitten. He giggled as the kittens began to crawl around in his lap.

Denny stood off to the side and watched the others.

"Why are the kittens all different colors?" he asked Grandpa.

"Because their relatives are all different colors," Grandpa answered. "When a mother and father that are from many different-colored relatives have a family, the kittens will be many different colors."

"I like the little calico kitten. It looks just like its mother," Denny said.

"That little kitten will be a mother someday, too. All calico cats are female. Calico females usually produce kittens that are a variety of colors," Grandpa explained.

"Let's go ride Bessie," Ty said, jumping up to leave. The rest followed him out of the hayloft to Bessie's stall.

Grandpa put a saddle and bridle on Bessie. Then he asked, "Who wants to ride first?"

"I do!" Ty said so loudly that Bessie jumped.

"Easy there, girl." Grandpa held Bessie as he helped Ty get onto the horse.

Bessie was a small, gray horse that had been with Grandpa for many years. The children had ridden her before when they had visited the farm. Bessie was very gentle with children and seemed to enjoy having them ride on her back.

Each child took a turn riding. Ty was told to ride slow and stay inside the barnyard so Grandpa could keep an eye on him.

When Ty was done, Audrey took a turn. She rode out of the barnyard and down the gravel road. She took a nice leisurely ride. When she returned, it was Jenny's turn.

"What took you so long?" Jenny asked.

"What's your hurry?" Audrey answered. "We've got all afternoon."

Jenny took a fast, short ride down the gravel road and over the bridge, and then she returned.

Denny was last. He got on Bessie and said, "Is it all right if I ride for a while, Grandpa? I'd rather ride Bessie than look at the bunny."

"Okay," Grandpa said. "You take as long as you want. I'll show the rest of the kids our newest pet."

The group wandered over to where the bunny was housed.

The bunny was a bit wild, so Grandpa held him firmly while the children petted the small rabbit.

"When he gets used to us, he won't be as frightened," Grandpa assured the children.

"What does he eat?" Ty asked.

"Mostly grass and sweet clover for now. He also likes different types of veggies. We'll give him a carrot now and then out of Grandma's garden when she isn't looking."

Grandpa winked at Ty.

The children laughed. They had a fun time touring the farm with Grandpa. They met Ulla the cow, the goose family, the chickens, and saw all the farm machinery in the large, rounded-steel Quonset building.

✳   ✳   ✳   ✳

At the supper table, the children told Grandma about Sheriff Whippert and the deer shootings, about the kittens, about riding Bessie, and about the bunny.

"What bunny?" Grandma looked with surprise at Grandpa.

"The cottontail from the garden," Grandpa replied between mouthfuls of mashed potatoes. "I put him into the small chicken coop—with the mesh-fence runway—that we don't use anymore."

"That rabbit was supposed to go back to the woods by the river."

"I know, but I thought taking care of the rabbit would be a good project for Ty. He's got to learn how to take care of livestock if he wants to live on the farm this summer."

Grandma dropped her discussion with Grandpa, because she knew he was right, and turned to Ty.

"What did you name the bunny?" she asked.

"I called him Cottontail," Ty said proudly.

"He's so lame," Denny interrupted. "Since Grandpa said the rabbit was a cottontail, Ty named him 'Cottontail.' He's got no imagination."

"Have too!" Ty protested.

"Have not!" Denny retorted.

"Enough already," Grandma interrupted. "Eat your vegetables."

"I've eaten my potatoes, but I don't like green beans," Denny responded, while Ty made a yucky face.

"Well, yucky or not, we're all going to help raise veggies this summer, and if we raise them, we eat them," Grandma said with determination in her voice. "Now, each of you take a radish and try it."

She passed the radish dish to Jenny.

The children could see the determination on Grandma's face, so they looked at Grandpa for help in pleading their cause—they did not want to try eating a radish.

Grandpa shrugged his shoulders.

"Sorry, kids, I haven't won an argument around here for forty years, so don't expect any help from me. Just do what Grandma says, and everything will be fine."

Grandpa took a big bite out of a radish and started chewing. The children looked at him with dread written all over their faces, staring in disbelief at the radish dish. Then they each took a radish, but no one ate more than a nibble. Grandma assured them that by the end of the summer they would like "veggies."

CHAPTER 4

▼

THERE'S NOTHING
TO DO!

The children came down to breakfast Friday morning one at a time. They had gone to bed exhausted the night before, so Grandma let them sleep in—but that would come to a halt today before it became a habit.

Grandma was making pancakes, so she fixed each of the children some pancakes and an egg. Only Audrey ate her egg.

No one said much at breakfast. After they were done eating, Grandma and Grandpa gathered the children into the living room for a briefing on the house rules.

"I don't know what the rules are at your homes, but here at our house, we have a set of rules that everyone follows. I've written these rules on a piece of paper and will read them to you, and then I will hang them on the refrigerator in case you forget."

The children were too weary to object, so Grandma started reading.

"Number one: Everyone is up for breakfast at 7:30. I don't want to make seven breakfasts every morning."

"What if we're not here at 7:30?" Denny asked.

"Then you'll wait until noon to eat lunch," Grandma answered, and continued.

"Number two: You will do your chores after breakfast, and then you can play until lunchtime."

"What if we don't do our chores?" Jenny asked, looking defiant.

"Then you can't go and play until you do, and you also won't eat lunch until you're done with your chores, unless you've been excused."

Grandma forged on.

"Number three: Lunch is served at 12:00 noon."

"What happens if we're late?" Audrey asked.

"Then you'll wait until supper to eat. Now, let me continue, please. Number four: After lunch, Grandpa and I take a nap, so you will play quietly around the house or in the yard."

"How long do you nap?" Ty asked sweetly.

"About an hour. Number five: After our naps, Grandpa and I will do some fun things with you, like fishing in the creek or baking some cookies. We'll even let you take turns deciding what you want to do, once you know what's available to do around here."

"I know what I want to do," Ty burst out, "I want to ride Bessie."

"That's so lame," Jenny said. "We can't all ride Bessie. What will the rest of us do?"

"We'll think of some things for everyone to do," Grandma said. "Don't worry, Jenny."

She continued. "Number six: Supper is at 6:00, unless I say otherwise."

"And if we're late for supper, we'll go to bed hungry," Audrey stated proudly.

"Yes, that's right." Grandma laughed and continued.

"Number seven: Bedtime is at 9:00 for Ty and 10:00 for everyone else. You'll be in your rooms at that time. If you can't sleep, you can read or visit quietly."

"Can I play my Game Boy?" Denny asked.

"That would be all right with us, if it's okay with Ty. Remember, he's your roommate, and you'll have to agree on things to do when you are in the room together."

Denny glared at Ty, and Ty grinned back. For the first time in his life, Ty had something Denny would want—his approval. It was a good feeling.

"Other chores will be done throughout the day when Grandpa and I ask you to do something. For doing your chores each week, you will get an allowance of five dollars per week, which you can spend on Saturday afternoon when we go to town to get groceries."

"Five dollars per week!" Denny and Jenny exclaimed at once. "We get more than that at home for doing nothing."

Grandpa spoke for the first time.

"We know," he said. "You're being overpaid at home. Besides, you're in a training program here right now. Just be thankful we're not charging you for all the training you'll be getting."

The children sat stunned. They got the picture. If they didn't work, they wouldn't eat, and if they didn't eat when Grandma said, and what Grandma fixed, they would starve. It all looked very gloomy at the moment. No one dared speak, because they were afraid there would be more rules made.

Jenny looked at Denny to see what he was thinking. She could see Denny was going to be defiant, too, so she asked, "What if we don't follow the rules?"

"Well," Grandma said sweetly, "Grandpa and I discussed that last night and felt that you would follow the rules, but just in case you don't, we'll have to take away your privileges, such as TV, games, allowances, going to town, etc. Let's just try this before we get all upset. Who knows, you may like learning some new chores and having something to do."

The room became eerily quiet.

"If there are no more questions, let's get started," Grandma said. "Ty and Denny, you go with Grandpa, and he'll start you on your chores, and Audrey and Jenny, you come with me. We'll do the dishes first, and then I'll teach you how to weed and hoe in the garden. Next week we'll switch chores so you all learn to do a variety of jobs."

*   *   *   *

Grandma sprayed the girls with mosquito spray, and they headed for the garden shed.

"Audrey, you grab a hoe," Grandma instructed her oldest granddaughter when they got inside the shed. "Audrey will learn to hoe this morning, and Jenny will learn to pick weeds. Tomorrow morning, we'll switch jobs."

First, Grandma showed Jenny and Audrey the difference between radishes and weeds, then the difference between onions and weeds. Radishes had large, broad leaves with one big red root. Onions had several thin, tube-like blades with a large white root. Jenny was to pick out all the weeds around the plants, while Audrey would hoe between the plant rows.

Next, Grandma showed the girls how to hoe by gliding along the top of the ground and cutting the weeds off just below the ground.

"You hoe toward yourself, putting the hoe about half an inch into the ground. Don't chop, just scratch the top surface of the earth," she advised her granddaughters.

The girls worked diligently for about fifteen minutes, and then Jenny began to complain.

"My back hurts from bending over."

"You'll get used to it," Grandma assured her. "I've been doing this for fifty years, and I'm still okay. You'll live."

Jenny let out a great puff of breath in disgust and continued weeding the onions.

Audrey hoed too close to some of the radishes and cut off some of the plant tops.

"I'm sorry, Grandma," she apologized. "I've killed some of your radishes."

"No you haven't, dear. The part we eat is under the ground. Just dig out the red roots with your hands when you're done, and we'll have them for lunch. Do be careful so you don't hoe out anymore."

After several breaks, the weeding and hoeing was completed for the day. Next, they all picked radishes and onions for lunch, then cleaned the produce under the water pump by the windmill.

"Thank you for the good work you did this morning," Grandma told the girls as they walked toward the house. "Now you can play until lunch—promptly at noon."

"Yay!" the girls shouted together, then ran off to their room for a rest.

Sitting on their bed in the room, Jenny said, "There's nothing to do around here but work."

"Oh, stop complaining!" Audrey rebuked her. "I'm going to relax and read a while—all that hoeing wore me out."

"I don't like to read!" Jenny replied sharply. "I'm going outside to swing."

"Good riddance," Audrey muttered, as she opened her latest *Harry Potter* book.

*   *   *   *

Ty and Denny had followed Grandpa outside to the barn. They went around the back of the barn first, to where the bunny was housed.

"Are you hungry, little feller?" Grandpa asked the bunny, who immediately scampered back into the chicken coop.

"I'll bet he's hungry," Ty said with sympathy.

"I'll bet he's scared of us," Denny added.

"He's probably both," Grandpa said. "Let's pick some of that sweet clover by the cow fence and give him some water in his dish. This will be Ty's job, so we'll have him do it."

Grandpa showed Ty how to get fresh water from the windmill pump and cut off sweet clover by the fence. After Ty had put the food and water into the bunny pen, they moved back quietly and sat down on the cow fence to see if the bunny would come out to eat. He did.

*   *   *   *

Grandpa put Ulla into her stall in the barn, then he got his stool and milk pail, sat beside Ulla near her utter, and then started milking her by squeezing her teats. The milk squirted out in big splats at the bottom of the pail.

"Wow!" Ty said. "That's cool. I didn't know that milk came out that way."

"Where did you think it came out, her butt?" Denny said in disgust.

"Now, Denny," Grandpa spoke slowly, "Ty has never seen a cow milked, so how should he know where the milk comes out?"

Grandpa milked a while, then said, "Denny, come and sit down on the stool and try your hand at milking."

Denny looked frightened.

"What if she kicks me?" he asked.

"Old Ulla hasn't kicked in years. I doubt she knows how to kick anymore. Now sit down."

Denny milking Ulla

Denny sat on the stool reluctantly. He grabbed two of the teats and tried to squeeze out some milk, but nothing came out.

"I can't do this," he whined, trying to get up.

"Sit down," Grandpa ordered. "You don't quit after one try. Here, I'll show you. Try squeezing the teat from the top down."

Grandpa demonstrated.

"Now you try it."

Denny tried again, and sure enough, a spurt of milk came out.

"Wow, that's awesome!" he said.

Denny's eyes shone in amazement. He continued milking slowly, one hand at a time, squeezing the milk out of the nipples—swish, swish—into the pail.

Grandpa let Denny work until he stopped and complained, "My arms are tired."

"Yes, it's tiring. If you do this all summer, you'll be much stronger when you get back home this fall. Rest a minute, then try again."

After several rests, and ten minutes of squeezing, Grandpa told Denny he'd done a nice job for his first time. Denny got up, and Grandpa sat down and finished stripping the milk from the teats.

Denny and Ty carried the pail of milk to the house, while Grandpa and Laddie followed. Grandpa set the pail of milk on the kitchen table.

"Now, you run outside and bring in Laddie's water dish, and we'll give him a milk treat. I'll also pour a little milk into a pitcher so you can feed the kittens in the barn."

The boys scurried off. Grandma smiled at Grandpa, who was grinning from ear to ear.

"I think you're enjoying this as much as the boys," she said.

"That I am." Grandpa winked at Grandma. "That I am."

Chapter 5

▼

Conspiracy

The broccoli-egg casserole Grandma had made for lunch didn't go over too well. All of the children tasted the casserole and then nibbled away like mice, sorting out the things they didn't like. Grandma could see that the children would never last until supper, so she offered them an alternative.

"Perhaps you would like to make yourselves a peanut butter sandwich to supplement your lunch," Grandma said, as she set the peanut butter jar on the table next to the bread.

Each child took two slices of bread and proceeded to put a thick layer of peanut butter on each slice. The children devoured Ulla's chilled milk with gusto, along with the sandwiches.

"I love peanut butter," Ty mumbled with his mouth full of sticky peanut butter.

"That's nice, dear. Now, don't eat too fast, or you'll choke."

Watching the children with their mouths full of sticky peanut butter reminded Abby of a riddle.

"How are good friends similar to peanut butter and bread?" she asked.

No one answered—they were all too busy eating—so Abby answered her own riddle.

"Because they always stick together."

Ty burst out laughing, which caused some of his food to spurt out of his mouth and fly across the table.

"Gross!" Jenny scolded him.

"Use your napkin to wipe up the mess, Ty," Grandma instructed.

She decided not to ask any more silly questions.

*   *   *   *

After lunch, the children decided to get the kittens from the barn to play with, while Grandma and Grandpa took their naps. In the shade of the big cottonwood trees in the backyard, the children played with the kittens and discussed their morning activities.

"Hoeing and weeding are no fun!" Jenny complained. "This is going to be a bummer of a summer."

"Hey, that rhymes," Denny teased.

"Not funny!" Jenny shot back.

"Oh, quit your fighting!" Audrey ordered, and then changed the subject. "Let's think of some things to do to make the summer more fun."

"There are no swimming pools, no movies, no summer sports, no clubs, no nothing out here," Jenny lamented.

"Maybe we could start a club of our own," Denny said halfheartedly.

Ty perked up. "Yeah," he said. "That would be great. We could have a pet club and include the kitties, the bunny, and old Laddie."

"That's so lame," Jenny said. "The dog would chase the kittens and eat the bunny."

"No, he wouldn't," Ty protested. "Laddie wouldn't do that—would he, Audrey?"

"I don't know, Ty. We're not going to try it. But maybe we could start a club. Maybe we could think of something to do in a club that would take up our time. Grandpa promised to take us fishing down by the creek when he wakes up. Learning how to fish could be an activity."

Denny spoke with a bit more enthusiasm.

"If we have a club it will have to be a secret," he said. "that's the only way clubs are any fun."

"How about a secret pledge?" Audrey asked.

"We could hold up our right hand and make a fist with our thumb between our middle and first fingers," Denny said while he demonstrated.

Jenny chimed in. "Yes, and we could say: 'I promise to follow the club rules and keep the club secrets, or I'll get kicked out by the other members.'"

"And then bring our fist down over our hearts to seal the pledge," Audrey said, putting her fist over her heart.

"And if we break the pledge, may a thousand red ants crawl up our armpits," Denny added.

Audrey laughed. "No violence! A promise can be kept without a threat. Besides, where would we find a thousand red ants?"

"In a red ant hill," Ty said innocently.

Audrey gave him a killer stare and said, "Let's take the pledge."

After the children took the pledge, Jenny spoke.

"Now what can we do that would be fun?"

"We could find out who's shooting the deer," Audrey suggested.

"Yeah!" Denny was now fully activated.

"How would we do that?" Jenny asked with enthusiasm.

Audrey started plotting their spying activities.

"We'll have to get Grandpa to take us fishing by the James River, and then, while some of us fish, the rest can snoop around and see what we can find," she said.

"Awesome!" Ty cut in.

But Denny rounded on him. "If you say one word about any of this to Grandma and Grandpa, we'll cut out your tongue," he said.

Ty jumped up and cupped his hand over his mouth.

"No, we won't," Audrey assured her little brother. "But you can't say a word of this to Grandma and Grandpa—promise?"

Ty took his hand off his mouth, gave Denny a defiant stare, and said, "I promise."

Having solved that problem, Audrey continued.

"If we have a club, we'll need to have a name and a secret code."

Audrey was racking her brains, trying to remember what the books she had read said about clubs.

"I've got a name," Ty bubbled, "The City Kid's Club."

Jenny scowled at Ty.

"That's so lame," she said.

"Is not." Ty pouted.

"How about the Peanut Butter Club?" Denny suggested. "It looks like we'll spend most of the summer eating peanut butter, and like Grandma said, 'Good friends stick together like peanut butter.' We'll have to stick together to pull this off."

"Good name," Audrey agreed with Denny. "Now, for a code—a secret code—that Grandma and Grandpa won't be able to figure out."

"We could wiggle our noses like they do on the *Bewitched* TV show. That would be a signal to meet," Jenny said.

"Good idea." Audrey smiled. "Now, where should we meet?"

"Bunnies wiggle their noses," Ty said calmly, still thinking about the secret code.

"That's it!" Denny shouted. "We could meet in the bunny's house behind the barn. No one could see us there."

"That bunny house is too small for us all to get into," Audrey reasoned.

"No, it's not," Jenny said, getting up off the grass and running toward the barn. The others quickly grabbed the four kittens and followed her.

$$* \qquad * \qquad * \qquad *$$

Cottontail heard them coming—laughing and shouting—so he scampered into his house. One by one, the children crawled through the small door and were soon sitting side by side inside the bunny's house. Cottontail had been trapped in the corner, where he sat trembling. The only person who could stand up in the house was Ty, but there was enough room for them to sit comfortably.

"It stinks in here," was Audrey's first comment.

"Well, hold your nose. You'll get used to it after a while," Denny advised her.

"No, I won't, but it will do. Grandma and Grandpa will never find us here. We'll be safe to plan our strategies."

They were busy discussing their spying techniques when they heard the dinner bell ringing loudly on the front porch of the house.

Earlier that day Grandma had told the children, "When the dinner bell rings, you come running—pronto—no matter where you are or what you're doing."

That was Grandma's way of checking up on them and making sure they were okay.

Denny jumped up and hit his head on the roof of the old chicken coop.

"Ouch!" he wailed.

"What a klutz," Audrey said. She shook her head and crawled out of the coop, followed by the others.

*   *   *   *

"Everyone ready to go fishing?" Grandpa asked when they were all up on the front porch.

"Yes," Ty answered enthusiastically, while the others clapped their hands loudly.

"Good. I've only got two poles, so some of you will watch while the others fish. I'll teach you two at a time how to bait the hook and cast the line. Everything is here."

Grandpa pointed to the fishing gear lying on the porch floor.

"Each of you grab something, and we'll walk down to the creek."

"Could we go fishing by the James River instead of the creek?" Audrey asked.

Grandpa paused a moment, shrugged his shoulders, and asked, "Why do you want to go down by the river? There are just as many fish in the creek since the rain."

"We'd like to see the river," Denny lied. "We've never seen the James River."

"I suppose that would be okay. What do you think, Abby?" Grandpa asked his wife.

"You'll all have to be more careful by the river. It's bigger, deeper, and swifter than the creek."

"We'll be careful," Jenny promised. "We can all swim—even Ty."

"Yes I can," Ty bragged proudly.

Grandma turned to her husband.

"Then, I suppose it's okay—this once," she said.

"You'll have to keep a sharp eye on them down by the river, Josh," she warned.

"Don't worry, I will," Grandpa promised.

He looked at the children.

"Load all this stuff into the back of my pickup, and we'll be off," he said.

The children hurriedly loaded the fishing poles, tackle box, net, bait can, and water pails into the old Ford pickup. The three oldest crawled into the bed of the pickup, while Ty and Laddie got into the front cab with Grandpa, and off they went down the dusty gravel road.

Pickup driving down the road, loaded to go fishing

CHAPTER 6

▼

FISHING OR WHAT?

Denny didn't like the idea of going exploring with Ty, but when Grandpa announced that the girls would be the first to fish, he had no choice.

"You'll be responsible for Ty," Grandpa said. "If anything happens to him, you'll be punished."

Denny frowned—but only for a moment, and then he asked Grandpa a question.

"Where were the deer shot?"

"I'm not sure," Grandpa answered. "Maybe down the river where the trees get thicker and there is a nice beach. Sometimes people hang out there. Why do you ask?"

"Just curious."

Denny shrugged his shoulders, trying to act nonchalant, as he started walking toward the beach area. Ty followed close behind him.

*   *   *   *

"Don't be afraid of the worms," Grandpa said to Audrey after he had instructed her to put one on the fishhook.

She stood frozen, looking at the small can full of worms. "They're so squishy."

Audrey's face made an awful frown as she wrinkled her nose in disgust.

"Just take one and put the head into the hook, then push the rest of the worm onto the hook. Here, I'll show you how," Grandpa offered.

"Won't that kill the worm?" Audrey asked.

"Yes, it will, but it's only a worm. Fish got to eat, you know."

"Ugh."

Audrey looked dismayed.

Jenny had been watching nearby. She was glad Audrey was first—baiting a hook was not her idea of fun. Besides, she'd rather be with the boys. After the boys disappeared over a small hill along the river's edge, she turned her attention to the fishing lesson.

"There you go," Grandpa praised Audrey. "You've got it."

"Well," Audrey beamed with pride, "I guess that wasn't so bad after all. I can't wait to tell Sandy. She's always bragging about the things she does. I'll bet she has never put a worm on a fishhook."

"I'll bet she hasn't either." Grandpa grinned and then asked, "Who's Sandy?"

"My best friend. I really like her, but she can be a pain now and then. She brags so much—"

"She's a snob," Jenny cut in, thinking about the last time she'd been with Audrey and Sandy, and the two older girls had ignored her completely.

Audrey defended her friend.

"No, she's not."

Grandpa intervened at that point in the conversation.

"Pay attention now, Audrey," he told her. "I'll show you how to cast your line off the end of this dock, and then you can try it."

Jenny walked back to the bank of the river and sat down.

Audrey watched Grandpa cast out the line. Then he handed the pole to her. Audrey put her pole behind her and quickly thrust it forward. The line shot way out into the water.

"Good shot!" Grandpa exclaimed with surprise. "You're a regular pro at this. Now, hang onto the pole tight, and if anything starts tugging on the line, yell, and I'll help you reel it in."

Grandpa looked for Jenny, who was sitting at the beginning of the dock where she'd gone when he and Audrey had started casting.

"You're next, little lady," he announced as he started walking toward shore.

Jenny got the hook baited quickly—she wasn't afraid of any worm—but it took her several tries to cast the line out. She got it caught on a low-hanging tree branch the first time she tried. On the third try, she got the job done.

It's best to have the two of them a distance apart, Grandpa thought. *I'd hate to see them get their lines tangled up.*

He walked to his pickup and got his old lawn chair out of the back, set it up on the dock between the girls, and waited patiently for a fish to bite. While Grandpa waited, he petted old Laddie, who was content to sit at his feet.

After a very short time, Audrey screamed, "Something's tugging on my line, Grandpa—come quick!"

Grandpa came running and took hold of the fishing pole to check the pull of the fish.

"I think you've got a pretty big one here. Now, don't get nervous—hang on. We'll reel him in slowly so we don't lose him. Keep your line tight. If he tries taking off on you, give him a little slack and then continue reeling him in."

Audrey and Grandpa worked together, and soon the fish was splashing in the water by the dock where they could see that Audrey had caught a nice-sized Northern.

"I'll hold the pole," Grandpa said. "You run and get the net and the water pail, Audrey."

It didn't take Audrey long. She stood next to Grandpa as he tried to scoop the fish out of the water with a big net.

"Look how big it is," she said excitedly.

"Wow!" Jenny exclaimed as she watched Grandpa and Audrey get the fish out of the water. "That's awesome. I hope I get one that big."

"Go back and watch your pole," Grandpa advised Jenny, "or you'll lose it."

Jenny went back to the pole she had left lying at the foot of the dock. She sat down on an old log and continued fishing, while Audrey put another worm on her hook.

Jenny fishing on a log

*   *   *   *

The boys had run along the river's edge, over a small hill, and down into a wooded area where the river got wider. Farther up the river they saw a nice beach with an old picnic table sitting in the middle of it.

"Look at that cool table," Ty said as they approached the beach.

After examining the table, he sat down on the wooden seat that was connected to the table.

"That table is a wreck," Denny said. "You'll get splinters if you sit there."

"No I won't," Ty answered defiantly.

"Suit yourself. I'm going to look for clues."

"Me too."

Ty got up to follow Denny.

Denny walked along the beach, kicking the sand. Ty copied his hero. After a few minutes of the fruitless search in the sand, they decided to get down on their hands and knees, and they crawled along the river's edge in the tall grass and rocks. It wasn't long before they got tired of that, too.

Denny went back to the table and sat down to rethink his strategy. Ty sat on the beach near the shore and dug up piles of sand.

Sometime later he called, "Denny, look what I found."

Denny went to inspect. Ty held a brass shell casing about two and a half inches long and a half inch wide.

"That looks like a bullet shell after it's been shot," Denny said.

Denny had seen empty shells when his dad did target practice in their backyard.

"Maybe it's from the gun of someone who's been shooting the deer."

"Wow! I found a clue," Ty said excitedly.

"Maybe. Where did you dig it up?"

"Right here."

Ty pointed beside one of his sand piles.

"That's about thirty feet from the table," Denny said. "Maybe someone was sitting at the table resting, spotted a deer by the water, and started running toward it, firing away. Maybe there are some clues on the table—like fiber of some kind."

Denny sometimes watched *CSI* on TV when his parents weren't home. He knew all about forensic tests. He checked for clues under the table but found none.

"Let's dig some more," Denny said to Ty.

Denny was excited now that they had found a clue. After digging another ten minutes, the boys found one more shell casing. It was just like the first one.

Denny put both casings into his pocket and said, "We'd better get back to the fishing dock. Grandpa will wonder what happened to us. Don't you say a word about these shell casings, Ty. It's our club secret."

"I won't," Ty promised, tagging along as fast as he could when Denny started running in the direction of the dock.

*   *   *   *

"Guess how many fish we caught!" Jenny shouted as the boys approached.

"One," Denny guessed.

"No, three. I caught the medium-sized one, and Audrey caught the big one and the little one. Look in the pail."

"Wow!" Ty exclaimed as he peered into the water pail and saw the fish tied up along the edge.

He jumped back.

"They're still wiggling!"

"Sure are," Grandpa laughed. "They won't be dead until I cut off their heads."

"Gross!" Jenny gasped.

"Can I fish now, Grandpa?" Ty asked.

"Sure. Audrey, why don't you hand him your pole, and you can take a break."

"Gladly," Audrey said as she handed her pole to Ty.

"Hang on tight," she instructed him, "and if you feel something pull, call Grandpa right away. Okay?"

"Okay," Ty said, gripping the pole firmly, with determination on his face.

"Are you ready to quit too, Jenny?" Grandpa asked.

"Sure."

"Wait just a minute," Denny told his sister. "I want to talk to Audrey before I start fishing."

Denny and Audrey walked to the shore and stood behind a large tree so no one could see them.

"Audrey, guess what?" Denny whispered. "We found a clue, I think."

"What was it?"

"Two gun shell casings."

"Awesome! Let me see."

Denny showed her the casings and explained where they had found the clues.

"That's great," Audrey said softly. "Jenny and I will go back there and see what we can find in that area. There might be some forensic evidence on the table. We studied about forensics in science class last year. That was cool. We'd better not sit at the table until we notify Sheriff Whippert, so we don't destroy any evidence."

"Let's not tell him yet," Denny whispered.

"We'll see," Audrey replied.

"Are you coming, Denny?" Jenny called from the dock.

"Right away," Denny shouted back and then looked at Audrey. "Good luck."

The two spies came out from behind the tree. Denny took Jenny's fishing poll, while the girls ran off in the direction of the beach.

Grandpa shook his head in curiosity as he watched them disappear over the hill.

Why so much excitement over a beach? he wondered.

CHAPTER 7

▼

MORE CLUES

Jenny and Audrey raced to the beach and were winded when they got there.

"Don't sit at the table," Audrey instructed Jenny.

"Why not?"

Audrey told Jenny what Denny had said when they were behind the tree by the dock.

Jenny's eyes grew wide.

"Wow, that's awesome!" she said. "Let's find some clues too."

The girls searched farther up the river along the shore. They walked through the tall grass and over the rocks.

They were about to turn back when Jenny shrieked, "I found a scarf, Audrey!"

Audrey ran to where Jenny was standing and looked at the dirty, weatherworn red scarf.

"I'm not sure that's a clue," she told Jenny. "This scarf looks like it's been here for ages, and the deer shootings have only gone on about a month."

Audrey put the scarf into her jeans pocket, then turned her attention to a cleared area about a hundred yards from where they were standing.

"Let's see what's over there," she said, pointing at the clearing.

Jenny ran to the spot Audrey was pointing out. The girls discovered that someone had made a campfire there, in an area that normally would have been covered with tall grass.

"It's dangerous to start a campfire out here," Audrey said, remembering her Girl Scouts camping rules. "Whoever did this was asking for a prairie fire—not a smart move."

"Why would they start a fire here?" Jenny asked.

"Maybe they didn't want anyone to see them on the beach. Although you can see a fire from here, there's so much tall grass around that you can't see any people who might be sitting here."

The girls explored the area and found some beer cans, candy wrappers, and a ticket stub from a movie.

"These are all clues," Audrey said, "but we'd better not touch them—just in case there are fingerprints."

Jenny nodded her head in approval while Audrey continued her planning.

"We'll tell Sheriff Whippert about this place in the morning," Audrey said. "Let's take the movie ticket stub and leave the rest. If it rains before the sheriff gets here, the stub could be ruined. Maybe if we gave the stub to the sheriff, he could find out what movie theater it came from and then see if any of the kids from that area have been here lately."

"That's a great plan, Audrey," Jenny said.

Audrey picked the ticket stub up carefully at the very tip of the paper. She was trying not to smudge any fingerprints that might be on it. She put the stub in her shirt pocket.

The girls continued walking along the shore and spied a heavily wooded area across the river, about a hundred yards from the riverbank.

"Doesn't it look like there's an old cabin up there?" Jenny asked, squinting to make out the shaded form in the woods.

"Yes, you're right," Audrey responded. "It does look like there's some sort of a building behind all those trees."

"Let's go see," Jenny said excitedly.

"How are we going to get across the river?"

"Swim," Jenny said.

Audrey protested.

"We'd get all wet. Grandpa wouldn't like that. He'd ask questions if we came back all wet."

"We could take off all our cloths and swim across naked."

"No way!" Audrey said, shocked. "I don't want anyone to see me running naked through the woods. What if someone is taking pictures? I'd be totally embarrassed."

Jenny stared at Audrey in disgust.

"Yeah, yeah, okay. We won't swim naked. We'll have to come out here sometime, alone, and bring our swimsuits."

"It's time to head back to the dock," Audrey said to change the subject. "Grandpa will worry if we take too long."

*   *   *   *

The boys were good at putting worms on the hooks—in fact, they enjoyed it. Denny put two worms at a time on his hook. He wanted to make sure the fish had plenty to eat.

The casting was easy for Denny, but Ty had a hard time mastering the skill. Grandpa showed Ty how to cast several times, then gave up and did the casting himself. He thought Ty might be too young to learn such a difficult skill.

After the line had been properly cast, Grandpa let Ty hold the pole while he sat close by with Laddie. He didn't want Ty to lose his best fishing pole to some ambitious fish.

By the time the girls got back, Ty and Denny had caught four average-sized fish. One was a Walleye.

As the girls approached, Ty yelled, "I caught a Walleye! Come see. Grandpa says Walleye are the best-tasting fish."

The girls looked in the large pail, which was almost full of fish.

"We'll have to head home soon," Grandpa said. "It's getting late, and there are chores to do. Ulla needs to be milked, and the bunny needs to be fed. Grandma can also use some help making supper. We'll clean the fish for supper behind the Quonset on my old worktable."

They loaded all the fishing equipment into the pickup bed, and the three older children climbed into the bed with Laddie. Grandpa drove slowly home along the bumpy gravel road.

"Did you find any clues?" Denny whispered to Audrey as they bumped along the road.

"Yes, we found a red scarf, some beer cans, candy wrappers, and a movie ticket stub. Here, I'll show you."

Audrey reached into her shirt pocket and pulled out the ticket stub. Then she reached into her back jeans pocket and took out the dirty red scarf.

"Great!" Denny said. "Those are good clues."

"We'll give them to Sheriff Whippert tomorrow."

"Let's wait," Denny pleaded.

"No, he needs to examine this stuff so he can solve the mystery and prevent more deer killings."

"Aww, you're no fun at all," Denny complained.

"We're not going to jail for withholding evidence," Audrey said firmly.

Jenny spoke up.

"I think Audrey's right. We'll go back sometime and find more clues. We want to stop the shootings as soon as possible."

Denny knew he was outnumbered, so he didn't say any more.

*   *   *   *

Cleaning fish was a messy affair. Grandpa made them all watch so they could learn to clean their own fish.

"You're all old enough to learn to filet a fish," he said as he took the first Northern out of the pail and cut its head off. Then he cut the fish's belly open from the tail to the throat and took out the insides. The girls gagged, and Ty covered his eyes. Only Denny thought that taking the insides out of a fish looked like fun.

Next, Grandpa cut the meat off the backbone on one side of the fish, starting at the throat and cutting as close to the bone as he could, all the way down to the tail. After that, he cut out the meat by running the sharp knife between the meat and the skin and being careful not to cut any of the skin. Last, he cut the ribs out along the bottom of the filet. When he was done with one side, he turned the fish over and did the other side.

"Run up to the house and get a clean pail from Grandma, then fill it full of cold water from the well," he instructed Audrey and Ty. "You other two stay and watch. I'll let you try filleting the next fish."

Audrey and Ty took off like a flash of lightning, while Jenny and Denny stood frozen in their spots.

With Grandpa's help and instructions, Denny did a good job filleting the next fish. Then it was Jenny's turn.

Jenny never could let Denny get the best of her, so she tried her hardest to show Grandpa she was as good as Denny at this task.

By the time Audrey and Ty got back with the water pail, all the fish except two were filleted.

"Put those fillets into the water pail and wash them good," Grandpa instructed the twins, "while I help Audrey do the last two fish. Ty, you watch. I think you're probably too little to have such a sharp knife in your hand."

Audrey wanted to prove to the others that she was a grown-up, so she took the fish filleting seriously and finished the last two fish in no time at all.

The children washed the fish in the pail, poured out the dirty water, and walked to the windmill to add fresh, cold water to the pail.

"You all did a great job today," Grandpa praised the children. "Now, you girls run these fillets up to the house so Grandma can fry them, while the guys and I milk Ulla."

*   *   *   *

The fish supper, with some French-fried potatoes, was delicious. The children ate heartily; they were hungry from their afternoon of fishing and finding clues. They even tried some of Grandma Abby's garden lettuce with her homemade ranch dressing. Ty ate three of Grandma's homemade buns with honey and peanut butter on them. For desert there was banana cream pie. The children ate until they were stuffed.

"Well … I see that you all eat just fine when you don't snack all day like you do at home," Grandma remarked after supper.

"We were starved," Jenny said.

"Good," Grandma replied. "From now on, Grandpa will starve you during the day, and you'll eat what's set in front of you at suppertime."

The children did not like the idea of no snacks during the day, but they were all too full to complain.

After supper, the children got to watch TV for an hour, and then they went to bed. It wasn't long before it was very quiet upstairs.

"They've had a big day," Abby remarked as she sat in her recliner crocheting.

Abby crocheting in her rocking chair

"Something's going on with that bunch," Josh said. "They were running around today looking for dead deer and whispering behind trees. I think they are looking for some clues to the killings."

"Well, let them look," Abby said nonchalantly, without dropping a stitch. "They need something to stimulate their minds. Let's see how creative they get. Just keep an eye on them, and make sure they don't do anything dangerous."

Josh nodded agreeably, then picked up his favorite farm magazine and began reading.

CHAPTER 8

▼

TELLING SHERIFF WHIPPERT

Saturday morning at breakfast, Audrey announced, "There's something we need to tell Sheriff Whippert."

Grandma stopped her pancake preparation, and Grandpa set down his cup of coffee.

"We're listening, Audrey," Grandpa said.

"We found some clues to the deer killings down by the river yesterday."

"What did you find?" Grandma asked.

"Some gun shells, a red scarf, and half a movie ticket."

Grandpa was impressed.

"Well. Sounds like quite a find. I'll call Sheriff Whippert after breakfast and have him come out to look at your clues."

"Now, eat your breakfast," Grandma instructed. "We've got some chores to do, then we'll go to Aberdeen for some groceries after lunch."

"Yay!" the children all shouted at once.

Grandpa held his hands over his ears. "Take it easy!"

"Sorry," Jenny said. "We're excited about going shopping. Do we get our allowance today?"

"You've worked half a week, so you get half your allowance," Grandma answered.

"Oh," Jenny muttered disappointedly.

"But," Grandma continued, "if there's a matinee at the theater in Aberdeen, we'll take in a movie for a treat."

"Yay!" the children all shouted again.

Grandpa gave the children a severe look. "Enough noise for one breakfast," he said. "Now eat!"

*   *   *   *

Grandpa phoned Sheriff Whippert after breakfast and asked him to stop by the farm as soon as possible. Then he gathered his workforce together on the porch and announced that the lawn would have to be mowed today before they left for Aberdeen.

The self-propelled push mower was stored in a small shed behind the house. After checking the oil, Grandpa started the mower and demonstrated how to run it. Then he gave each child a portion of the yard around the house to mow.

"We know how to mow, Grandpa," Denny said. "We've all mowed our lawns at home—even Ty."

Ty nodded vigorously, with a big grin on his face.

After the hand mowing was done, they all went down to the Quonset, where the riding mower was stored.

Denny's eyes lit up when he saw the green and yellow tractor mower. "This will be fun," he said.

"We'll let you go first," Grandpa told Denny. "Get on, and I'll show you how to start John."

"Why do you call the mower John?" asked Ty.

"Because this is a John Deere mower—the very best," Grandpa replied.

Grandpa showed Denny how to put his foot on the clutch-brake, set the throttle, and turn on the ignition key to start the mower. After it started, he told Denny to put the lever out of park and set the speed control, and then put the mower into drive.

"Now, slowly release the clutch-brake," Grandpa instructed.

Denny released the clutch too fast, and the mower jerked forward, shuddered, and then suddenly stopped.

"I guess we'll have to try that again," Grandpa said calmly.

On the next try, Denny got the mower moving forward slowly. Everyone followed Denny and the mower as they exited the garage.

After they were out on the grass by the barn, Grandpa decided to demonstrate before he let any of the children cut grass with the riding mower.

"You set the blade on low, slowly release the clutch, and watch where you're going. I'll make a round, and then you'll have something to follow."

Grandpa driving the mower beside the Quonset

The children watched Grandpa make the first swath around a large patch of grass, and then it was Denny's turn to try. He made several rounds and did a nice job.

Jenny was next. She had been watching carefully. It was a little hard for her to manage the blade lever and the clutch at the same time, but she was determined, and she struggled until she got it right. When her turn was over, she put the blade out of action and the drive lever into neutral. Then she got off the mower.

"Wow, that was great—I love to drive," she beamed.

Audrey took to the mower like a duck takes to water. She got everything right the first time. Audrey liked to drive anything with wheels on it. She got to drive her dad's golf cart once in a while when he went golfing. She was looking forward to getting her driver's permit in a few years.

"I'm next," Ty shouted over the roar of the motor as Audrey dismounted.

"I should probably drive with you," Grandpa suggested to Ty. "You're too little to handle the clutch and levers at the same time."

Grandpa got on the mower, and Ty sat on his lap. With Ty steering and Grandpa doing the rest, they finished cutting the grass around the barn and Quonset. Then they rode the mower to the garden area and made the first round around the garden and down to the creek.

Sheriff Whippert's car appeared on the bridge as Grandpa and Ty pulled up in front of the other children to change drivers. Grandpa turned off the mower and waited for the sheriff's car to pull up in front of them.

Sheriff Whippert rolled down his window.

"Hey there, Josh," he said. "Got your message—what's up?"

Audrey stepped forward and spoke up boldly.

"We were out fishing yesterday by the James River with Grandpa. While two of us were fishing, the other two went exploring. We found some clues to the deer shootings."

The sheriff looked surprised.

"Well, how about that," he said.

Audrey reached into her pocket and pulled out the two shell casings, the red scarf, and the movie ticket stub.

"Here," she said as she handed the clues to the sheriff.

"These look interesting," Sheriff Whippert said, "especially the shell casings. I'll take them to the lab and have them examined. Maybe they will match the bullets that were inside the dead deer. Exactly where did you find these?"

"I dug them up in the sand on the beach by the table," Ty burst out.

"Well, little feller, you done good," the sheriff complimented Ty.

Denny added, "The shooters may have been sitting on the table or hiding under the table when they shot the deer. Maybe they left some fiber or hair or fingerprints on the table."

"Maybe they did," Sheriff Whippert said with a chuckle.

The sheriff examined the scarf and ticket stub.

"I doubt that these clues will prove useful, but I'll take them in anyway," he said.

Audrey had more information to share.

"There were also some beer cans and candy wrappers lying around a campfire about a hundred yards south of the table," Audrey said. "We didn't touch any of that stuff, because we didn't want to destroy any DNA evidence you might find."

"Good thinking," the sheriff said. He seemed pleased with what the children had found. "You kids are really good detectives."

The children beamed with pride.

"Maybe we'll be able to stop the deer shootings," Jenny speculated.

"Maybe we will," the sheriff agreed. "I'd better get down to the river and find those cans and wrappers before they blow away. See you later, Josh—kids."

Sheriff Whippert drove away, waving good-bye.

*   *   *   *

It took Denny, Jenny, and Audrey another two hours to complete all the mowing, but they finished in time for lunch.

They all hurriedly gobbled their food and got ready for the ride to Aberdeen. Grandma had looked up the movies that were showing during the afternoon, and they decided to go see a movie about a horse, called *Seabiscuit.*

They stopped at Wal-Mart first and spent their $2.50. Ty bought a coloring book because he loved to color and draw. Jenny bought some butterfly hair clips to keep the short hair out of her eyes when she put the rest of her hair up in a ponytail. Denny got a new card game he could play with Grandpa and Ty when TV got boring after supper. Audrey bought a book that was on sale. Her favorite thing to do, when she had free time, was read. Grandma and Grandpa picked up some household supplies.

*   *   *   *

"That was good," Audrey said as they left the theater and walked to the car. "Thanks for the popcorn and soda, Grandpa."

"You're welcome," Grandpa said. "I'm glad you enjoyed it."

Jenny joined the conversation.

"I love horses," she said, thinking about the beautiful racehorse in the movie.

"It would be fun to be a jockey," Denny thought out loud.

Ty asked, "Do you suppose we could make a racehorse out of Bessie?"

Everyone laughed.

"I don't think so, Ty," Grandpa chuckled. "Bessie's racing days are long gone."

"We'll pick up a few groceries and head for home," Grandma said as they got into the car. "We need to get the chores done before supper, and I also need to fix a hot dish for church tomorrow. There's a picnic after the eleven o'clock service."

"Church?" Denny questioned in surprise. "We don't go to church in the summer, because there's no Sunday school."

"There is in our church. And even if there wasn't, you'd go anyway," Grandma stated firmly. "Giving up a few hours a week to learn about religion isn't asking too much."

The children sat quietly and looked at one another. They were beginning to understand the family structure they were living in; Grandma and Grandpa were in charge, and the kids did what they were told to do.

CHAPTER 9

▼

CHURCH PICNIC

Denny continued eating as if he didn't hear Grandma, who was delivering the day's rules to everyone at breakfast.

"You'll all sit quietly and listen to Pastor Bender's sermon. There's no Sunday school today, only a church picnic after the service."

"What's a church picnic like?" Ty asked.

"It's fun—you'll see," Grandpa responded. "There's lots of good food, and we all play games after we eat."

"What kind of games?" Jenny wanted to know.

"We usually play softball until we're tired of that, then there's volleyball for those who still have energy left after the softball."

"I like softball," Ty said with zeal. "I—"

"Good," Grandma interrupted. "Now finish your breakfast and get dressed. Be sure to wear casual clothes so you can play games after lunch."

*   *   *   *

Country church

Pastor Roy Bender cut the church service short when the place started humming like a beehive—the children were getting restless. There were more children in church today than usual because of the annual Sunday school picnic.

After the service, everyone went down to the basement and got in line for lunch. The children filled their plates, gobbled their food, and went outside to play.

The four Haskell grandchildren felt out of place. They stood by themselves watching the others play softball.

Pastor Roy Bender, who had been introduced as Pastor Roy to the Haskell's grandchildren when they came into the church before services began, walked over to where the children were standing.

"I'll bet you're all good softball players," he said.

Ty piped up with confidence.

"We sure are!" he said.

Pastor Roy laughed, and then shouted over the roar of the baseball game.

"Who needs some good ball players?" he called.

"We do," Randy Cavett answered.

Randy was Elmer and Emma's grandson. He had dark hair that he wore a little too long. His Native American heritage was evident in his facial features.

"All right," Pastor Roy said. "Denny and Jenny can join Randy's team, and Ty and Audrey can join Gretchen's team. We'll put you out in the field to start with; then we'll all take turns playing different positions."

The spirited game continued with much shouting and laughing. Everyone "oohed" when Audrey hit a home run. Denny and Jenny both got base hits when they were up to bat. Ty struck out. He walked to the bench with tears in his eyes.

At that point in the game, Pastor Roy, who had seen Ty strike out, volunteered to pitch for both sides. All the children cheered. They liked him.

Pastor Roy was a young minister in his midtwenties, and he had just recently married. The young families in the church loved him and his friendly wife, Irene.

"Strike her out," Randy shouted to Pastor Roy when it was Audrey's turn to bat. Randy wasn't too happy when Audrey had hit a home run the last time she'd batted. Randy was a very competitive and good player. He didn't like girls doing better than he did in any sport.

Audrey whacked the ball way out into the field, and Jenny picked it up and threw it home, but not in time to put Audrey out. Audrey had cleared the bases with her hit. This was not good for Randy's team.

Ty was up next.

"Strike him out," Randy shouted to Pastor Roy.

Pastor Roy pitched a really slow ball to Ty so he could hit it. Ty swung and missed. Pastor Roy could see the disappointment on Ty's face.

"Hold your bat out a little more," the Pastor instructed.

Ty did as he was told. Pastor Roy pitched again and tried to get the ball to hit the bat, but Ty moved the bat too soon and missed the ball again. Now he was very close to more tears.

"Hold your bat still," Pastor Roy suggested.

The children saw Pastor Roy look up to heaven; he looked as if he was praying. Then he aimed very carefully and threw very precisely.

Whack, went the bat. Ty hit the ball into left field and started running to first base.

"I did it—I did it!" Ty howled and jumped up and down on first base.

Pastor Roy grinned, looked up to heaven, and whispered, "Thanks."

To the delight of all the young players, the adults joined the game after they finished their lunch. The game became more spirited with the adults playing. The laughter increased when the older players struck out, dropped a ball, or stumbled while running the bases.

Elmer and Grandpa Josh decided to join in the fun. Elmer joined Randy's team, and Grandpa went out into the field on Gretchen's team. The first time at bat, Elmer hit the ball into left field where Grandpa was standing. Grandpa picked up the ball and fired it home to Irene, who was catching. Grandpa had thrown the ball so hard that Irene couldn't catch it; Elmer scored a run.

"Just lucky," Grandpa Josh shouted at Elmer, as his friend, in total exhaustion, went to sit down.

"Just *good*," Elmer shouted back, then laughed. "We'll see how good you do when it's your turn."

When it was Grandpa's turn at bat, he hit the ball out into right field. However, he only made it to first base—he didn't run very fast, because of the rheumatism in his knees. He was thankful he made it that far.

"I need a pinch runner," he shouted from first.

"I'll run for you, Grandpa," Ty volunteered and headed for first.

"Thanks."

Grandpa patted Ty on the head when he got to first. "I appreciate that."

The game continued with gusto until two o'clock, when the church ladies brought lemonade and cookies outside for the team players to take a break.

Ty filled his glass to the brim and gulped down the cool lemonade. He had worked up quite a thirst running the bases. Pastor Roy had made sure that Ty hit the ball every time he came up to bat, and since Ty also ran the bases for Grandpa Josh, he had to run twice as much as the other players. He loved every minute of it and felt like a real team hero.

When all the lemonade and cookies were gone, the game continued for another half hour. Then someone suggested they all play volleyball, so the group divided into two teams and continued their competition.

Denny and Randy had become friends while they were playing softball, so they stayed on the same team for volleyball. Although the two boys were both thin, Randy was a few inches taller, and his dark hair and brown eyes contrasted with Denny's blond hair and blue eyes. One thing they had in common was their competitive spirit. They played to win.

Denny and Randy complimented each other when they made a good play. They also gave each other a high five when they scored. The boys had lunch together before they went home. They were becoming good friends.

✳　　✳　　✳　　✳

At four, Grandpa and Grandma loaded the kids and leftover food into the car and drove home. The children were eager to share their afternoon experiences.

"I met this girl about my age, whose name is Missy," Jenny said excitedly. "She said she was Randy's sister and lives about half a mile from your farm, Grandpa."

"Randy and Missy are Elmer and Emma's grandchildren," Grandpa said. "They live with their grandparents because their mom and dad are divorced. Their dad works for the railroad and is gone most of the time."

Audrey asked, "Where's their mom?"

Grandma answered. "She left several years ago to find herself. She hasn't come back … so sad for the children," she said with a sorrowful look on her face.

"I like Randy," Denny said. "He's really a good athlete. He can run like the wind."

"He has inherited that from his grandfather and dad, who were both excellent runners," Grandpa said. "I know—I never could beat Elmer in a footrace."

"Can they come over and play sometime?" Denny asked.

Grandpa looked at his wife.

"You'll have to ask Grandma," he said.

"Sure." Grandma smiled. "Maybe next Sunday after church. That can be the reward if you all behave and get your work done this week."

"We will," Ty beamed. "I love to play softball."

CHAPTER 10

▼

THE DESPICABLE GOOSE

Except for exchanging chores—the girls learned to milk Ulla, and the boys learned to hoe and weed the garden—the routine on the farm proceeded as usual until Thursday, when Ty learned not to tease the geese.

Grandma had warned the children about the gander; he could be mean if provoked. Ty ignored the geese entirely until Thursday morning, when he got bored after he had finished his chores.

After Ty fed Cottontail, he noticed the geese resting in the shade by the barn. He just had to go over and roust them up.

At first, the geese didn't move. All ten of them—a mother goose, the gander, and eight little goslings—sat still and stared at Ty.

How dare they ignore me, Ty thought. *I'll show those stupid geese who's boss.*

Ty walked over to the front of the Quonset, where there was a variety of gravel stones, and picked up a handful of the larger pebbles.

I'll show those geese who's in charge around here.

He walked around the corner of the barn, where the geese were still resting peacefully, and shouted, "Get out of here, you dumb geese!"

The geese got up but didn't go anywhere. They seemed to be wondering why they had to move. It was so nice and cool behind the barn away from the hot sun.

Ty began throwing the pebbles at the geese, mostly at the gander, who stood in defiance in front of his family.

The mother goose and goslings started to run to escape Ty's pelting. The gander stood firm.

Ty got braver. He walked closer to the gander and threw the last pebble he had right at the gander's head. It hit the gander between the eyes.

That did it! The gander spread his wings, started making a hissing noise, and ran toward Ty.

Ty was out of pebbles, so he took off toward the Quonset, chased by the gander, to get some more ammunition.

When Ty reached the Quonset, he quickly bent over to pick up some more pebbles.

The gander, which was determined to stop Ty's unprovoked assault, bit Ty on his bottom as he bent over.

"Ouch!" Ty screamed, and took off for the house. At this point in the conflict, Ty could see he was no match for the irritated gander. The race was on.

Grandma Abby was on the porch sweeping up the mess the kids had made the night before when they had all eaten supper outside. She heard the noise.

"Lord above," she said out loud, "what's going on?"

She looked toward the Quonset and saw Ty running and screaming with the gander in close pursuit.

Ty being chased by the gander

Grandma, with the broom firmly in hand, headed toward the screaming child. As Ty ran past her, she whacked the gander on his chest and sternly said, "Stop that!"

The gander stopped abruptly and looked with surprise at Grandma. Then he turned and headed back to his family, who were peeking around the edge of the barn.

Grandma walked toward the house and up the front step. She found Ty sitting on the porch swing, a little shaken.

"Serves you right," she said. "I told you not to provoke the geese—or any other animal, for that matter. They will defend themselves, you know."

"I'm sorry," Ty said meekly. "I didn't mean any harm."

"How did you get him so angry?" Grandma asked.

"I threw some small pebbles at him—that's all."

"That's all?" Grandma asked in a harsh voice. "That's enough! I don't want you ever to throw anything at any animal on this farm. That's not very nice."

"I'm sorry," Ty said again and hung his head.

"I think the gander has taught you a lesson, so I won't punish you—this time. If it happens again, there will be a penalty for such rude behavior."

Ty hung his head and went inside the house and upstairs to his room. He needed to rest after his frightening ordeal.

*   *   *   *

The children had their third meeting of the week in the Peanut Butter Club house on Friday, while Grandma and Grandpa took their naps.

Cottontail was getting used to having his living quarters invaded by the four Haskell grandchildren several afternoons a week. He sat quietly in Jenny's arms while the children talked.

Audrey started the meeting on a sad note.

"I read the *Gazette* this morning, and there was another write-up about the deer shootings. It said that Sheriff Whippert hasn't found the poachers yet."

"I think he's lazy," Denny remarked. "He never gets out of his car. I'll bet he hasn't even checked out the clues we've given him."

"I'll bet he hasn't either," Jenny chimed in. "We'll have to solve this mystery ourselves."

"Yeah, sure," Audrey said.

She looked at the twins in disbelief as she shook her head.

"And if we discover who's doing the shooting, we just walk up to him and arrest him? Remember, he's got the gun."

Ty looked frightened.

"Audrey's right. He's got the gun to shoot the deer," he repeated.

"Okay," Denny agreed, "but what can we do?"

"Let's investigate the cabin in the woods," Jenny suggested while petting Cottontail. She had been wondering about the cabin since she and Audrey had spotted it a week ago.

"Yeah!" Ty shouted so loudly that he frightened Cottontail, who struggled to get away from Jenny so he could go hide somewhere away from the noise.

Denny grabbed Ty by the throat.

"Stop that yelling!" he said. "You're scaring the rabbit. Someone might hear you."

"Like who?" Audrey questioned. "Grandma and Grandpa are sleeping, and there's nobody else around."

"All right. Let's talk about the cabin," Denny said.

"It looked like an old, abandoned cabin," Audrey said. "I doubt there are any clues in it."

"We could go up there on Sunday and investigate. Maybe the Cavetts can come with us, if they're here," Jenny suggested.

"Cool," Denny added. "Randy said he knows a lot about the woods and tracking animals and things like that. Maybe he could help us find clues."

"Maybe he's just bragging," Audrey speculated.

"Maybe," Jenny said, "but we won't know until we try. Let's do it. Please, Audrey."

Audrey considered Jenny's suggestion. "There are lots of maybes here. First, the Cavetts have to be here, then we have to figure out how to get Grandma and Grandpa's permission to go alone to the James River, and then we need to figure out how to get there—it's two miles, you know."

"Maybe Grandma won't let us have the Cavetts over," Jenny lamented. "She was pretty mad at Ty when he teased the geese."

"She's okay with that now," Ty piped up. "She told me she wasn't going to punish me, as long as I didn't do it again."

"Well, you'd better not screw up again this week, squirt," Denny warned, "or I'll punch you out."

"Stop that violent talk, Denny," Audrey said. "If you beat Ty up, we won't be able to have any privileges around here for weeks."

"Yeah, Denny, stop that violent talk," Ty repeated.

Denny ignored Ty and made a suggestion.

"Maybe we could get the Cavetts to ride their horses over here. Randy told me that he and Missy each has a horse. Then, we could get Grandpa to saddle up Bessie, and with six kids and three horses, we could ride double. We could tell Grandma and Grandpa that we're just going for a ride."

"That sounds like a good plan," Audrey said. "You can ride with Randy, Jenny can ride with Missy, and I'll ride Bessie along with Ty."

"That's going to be fun—riding—and maybe we'll find some more clues," Jenny said excitedly.

"Now," Audrey warned, "we'll all have to be super good until Sunday, so we can have those privileges. Let's do our club's secret sign and pledge."

The children all put up their right hands and made a fist with their thumbs between their middle fingers and index fingers. All together they said, "I promise to follow the club's rules and keep the club's secrets, or I'll get kicked out by the other members." Then they brought their fists down over their hearts to show their loyalty.

CHAPTER 11

▼

HORSING AROUND

On Sunday morning, the children were dressed for church and waiting on the front porch for Grandma and Grandpa.

When Grandpa came out the front door, Audrey asked, "Can the Cavetts come over after church today?"

"You'll have to ask Grandma," Grandpa replied.

The children looked at each other with somber faces. They knew that Grandpa was quicker to grant favors than Grandma was.

"Well, I see everyone is ready," Grandma spoke cheerily as she stepped out the door. "Let's go."

"Grandma," Audrey said politely, "can we have Randy and Missy over after dinner today?"

To the children's surprise, Grandma answered, "I guess that would be okay."

Their faces lit up at her reply.

"You've done all your chores this week, and you've even tried some of the veggies on your plates, so I think you deserve a reward."

"Yay!" Ty shouted.

Grandpa held his ears and looked solemnly at Ty.

"We'll make it a mini party," Grandma suggested, "to celebrate the end of your second week on the farm. I'll bake some brownies while you play. We'll also have some home-made ice cream and cold lemonade. Grandpa can make the ice cream while I bake the brownies."

"Yay," the children said together in a whisper. Then they all laughed, because this time Grandpa didn't have to cover his ears.

"I'll talk to Emma at church to make sure it's okay with her," Grandma said.

"Can they bring their horses, so we can go riding?" Denny asked. "We'll use Bessie, too."

Grandpa joined the conversation as they walked to the car and got in.

"That sounds okay," he said.

"I can hardly wait," Ty said happily as he buckled up his seat belt.

$$*\quad*\quad*\quad*$$

The children didn't hear a word Pastor Bender said, because they were anxious to get outside and talk to Randy and Missy about their plans to visit the mysterious cabin.

After church, while Grandma Abby talked to Emma, the Haskell's grandchildren huddled together by the Cavetts' car relaying their plans to Randy and Missy.

"Don't forget to wear your swimsuits," Denny whispered as the children parted to go to their own cars.

*   *   *   *

The children hurriedly gobbled down Grandma's home-made chicken noodle soup and egg salad sandwiches. Then they ran upstairs to change out of their Sunday clothes and put on old clothes to play in. They put on their swimsuits under their clothes. Jenny's shirt was so thin you could see her swimsuit through it.

"You'll have to wear you summer jacket over that shirt, or Grandma will see your swimsuit and ask where you're going," Audrey advised.

"That would be dorky on such a hot day."

"Dorky or not, you'd better do it, or all our plans will be ruined."

Jenny agreed reluctantly.

Next, the children met in the barn to saddle up Bessie, and then they waited for the Cavetts to come. It seemed like an eternity before they saw Randy and Missy riding down the road at a distance. As the Cavetts drew closer, they could see that Randy was riding a Paint pony with black patches, and Missy was riding a Paint pony with brown patches.

When the riders had crossed over the bridge, the Haskells went to meet them.

"What's the name of your pony?" Jenny asked Missy when the pony stopped in front of her.

"Blossom," Missy replied shyly.

Missy sitting on Blossom

Jenny petted Blossom on her nose and softly said, "Pretty Blossom. I like her, Missy—she's awesome."

Missy beamed.

"Thanks. You can ride with me."

Denny got up on Randy's pony, Jasper, and sat behind Randy, who was in the saddle. Audrey and Ty got Bessie from the barn, and the three horses and six children started slowly up the old gravel road that led to the James River.

*   *   *   *

It was a beautiful, warm summer day. They talked and laughed as they rode along slowly. They were in no hurry to get to the river. Grandpa had said to be back by four, so they had lots of time since it was only one o'clock.

The riders stopped to rest in the shade of some old cotton-wood trees.

"You guys want to belong to our Peanut Butter Club?" Denny asked Randy.

"What's a Peanut Butter Club?"

"It's a club where we have meetings and try to do fun things," Denny replied.

"Sounds neat," Missy said.

Denny told them, "All you have to do is take the pledge that everything we do is secret and you won't tell anyone."

"What's the pledge?" Missy asked.

Jenny held up her right hand, made a fist, and said, "I promise to follow the club's rules and keep the club's secrets, or I'll get kicked out by the other members."

Denny demonstrated while explaining.

"Then you bring your right fist down over your heart to show your loyalty—that's it."

"That's easy," Randy said as he held up his right hand and took the pledge. Missy did the same.

"Good!" Audrey said. "Now you're members. We'll have lots of fun this summer."

*   *   *   *

The six club members rode past the fishing dock and along the riverbank until they reached the beach with the picnic table.

"We could tie our horses to that table," Audrey suggested. "Then we could sneak up to the cabin while hiding in the tall grass. That way, if someone is in the cabin, they won't see us spying on them."

"Sounds good," Randy agreed. "I've been in that old cabin before, and it's pretty beat up. I doubt that anyone is living there."

The children got off their horses, tied them to the table, and started walking in the direction of the cabin.

Coming over the crest of the last hill, they could see the shack in the distance, partially hidden by the trees.

"Let's crouch down now, so no one can see us coming," Denny said.

Randy took the lead and stooped over in the tall grass. He moved forward slowly, followed by the others. When they were directly across the river from the cabin, Randy peeked up out of the grass and whispered, "There's a motorcycle parked in front of the cabin. Someone is there."

The other children peeked out of the grass, and sure enough, there was a big, black Indian Chief cycle parked in front of the old shack.

Motorcycle in front of cabin

"What if they've got a gun?" Ty whined. "They might think we're deer and shoot us."

"If you're not quiet, they will hear us, and then they will shoot us," Denny scolded him.

Jenny shushed them.

"Quiet! Both of you. We should lay low and watch for a while to see if anyone comes outside," she said.

The children sat in the tall grass and whispered to each other, taking turns sticking their heads up to see if anyone came out of the cabin.

"Someone is coming out," Audrey announced as she peeked over the grass. "It's a man with long hair in a braid. He's big and mean-looking."

"Is he alone?" Randy asked.

"So far," Audrey replied.

"Has he got a gun?" Ty inquired with wide eyes.

"Let me see." Jenny pulled Audrey down and popped her head above the grass.

"I don't see a gun," she assured Ty.

They heard the motorcycle start, so they peeked through the grass to watch the stranger get on his Indian Chief and drive away.

"Whew." Ty let out a puff of air in relief. "He looked mean, but I didn't see a gun."

"If he's going to shoot deer, he'll probably wait until night, so no one sees him. Maybe his gun is in the cabin," Audrey speculated.

As the motorcycle faded into the distance, Randy started taking off his clothes.

"Let's go," he said, "I want to see what's inside. The river is narrow and shallow here, so it's not hard to swim—I've done it before. In fact, there was an old bridge here once, but it's washed away now."

The three boys hurriedly took off their clothes and went into the river to swim across. When they reached the other side, Randy shouted to the girls to hurry.

"Don't be such sissies," he teased.

The girls took the challenge and rushed into the water and had a race to see who could get across first. Audrey won, but not by much. Missy and Jenny were good swimmers.

They all stood in front of the cabin dripping wet.

"We'll have to wait until we dry off a bit," Audrey observed, "or he'll know we were in the house if we make tracks and drip water everywhere."

The children walked around outside for a while, until they were dry.

"Let's go inside," Denny said. "I'm anxious to see what's in there."

"The front door is open," Randy announced as he turned the knob.

Jenny said, "It's so rickety that you probably couldn't lock it."

The children followed Randy into the one-room cabin. The floor had been swept recently, but the walls were dirty and full of spiderwebs. There was an old, broken-down table in the center of the cabin. It looked like it had been cleaned recently, except for the ashtray full of cigarette butts on the table. Two wobbly, old chairs sat near the table with towels and a washcloth hung on them to dry. The fireplace against the north wall had ashes in it. There was a folding cot in the corner with a large duffel bag nearby.

"It looks like someone is camping out here," Jenny said. "I don't see any food or supplies, so he must go somewhere to eat. Maybe he just comes here at night to shoot deer."

Missy looked frightened as she spoke. "Maybe he just comes here at night to shoot deer?" Since Missy didn't talk much, everyone looked at her in surprise.

"Maybe," Audrey agreed.

"Let's see what's in the duffel bag," Randy urged.

"No, we'd better not snoop," Audrey protested, but before the words were out of her mouth, Denny and Randy had the bag open and were peering inside.

Denny said, "We'd better not move anything, or he'll know someone was looking inside his bag."

The boys looked at the different things in the bag—underwear, socks, soap, toothpaste and brush, and a pistol.

Randy looked surprised when he spotted the pistol.

"Wow!" he said. "This pistol looks awesome."

"Don't touch that," Audrey warned as she looked inside the bag. "It could be loaded, and you'll put fingerprints on it."

"I hear a noise," Missy whispered.

The boys quickly zipped the bag as the girls headed toward the door.

"We'd better get out of here before he comes back," Jenny said. "He looked like a mean dude to me. I wouldn't want to get shot."

"Shot?" Ty shrieked as he grabbed Audrey's arm.

"We won't get shot," Audrey assured him, "but we'd better leave quick. We'll tell Sheriff Whippert about this in the morning."

As the children ran for the river, Randy protested.

"No, we won't," he said. "He won't do anything about it anyway."

"Yes, we will!"

These were Audrey's final words as she dove for the water and started swimming with all her might.

*   *   *   *

When they arrived back at the farm, the Haskell grandparents were waiting for them on the porch.

"How was the ride?" Grandpa asked as they got off their horses.

"Awesome," Jenny answered. Then she added, "You should get some of those Paint Indian ponies, Grandpa. They are really neat."

"I can only ride one horse at a time," Grandpa answered. "Bessie is good enough for me. Grandma doesn't ride."

"Never have," Grandma agreed. "I'm a city girl. Now get cleaned up before the ice cream all melts."

Ty burst out, "We're starved from our exciting adventure—"

Denny quickly clamped his hand over Ty's mouth.

"Come on, squirt, let's wash. I'm hungry," Denny said as he dragged Ty inside the house while the rest followed.

"I wonder what adventure they had that Denny didn't want us to know about," Abby asked, looking at Josh.

"Who knows," Josh said slowly, and shrugged his shoulders. "They've been down by the river again. I could smell the river water on their clothes and hair as they walked by. I suppose they'll tell us about it in the morning. If not, we'll have to beat it out of them."

Josh chuckled.

"Now, Josh, quit teasing. Thank God they're all home safe and sound. I worry about them at that river."

"Don't fuss so, Abby," Josh said. "God looks out for fools and children. They qualify as both."

CHAPTER 12

▼

THE CHICKEN CHALLENGE

Feeding the chickens and gathering the eggs were not Jenny's favorite chores, but for some reason, Grandma had stuck her with those jobs.

She was mumbling to herself as she walked to the chicken coop.

"This morning I'll show that old cluck who's boss," she muttered out loud. "I'll get her eggs by hook or by crook."

Every day since Jenny had been put in charge of the chicken chores, she had to get Grandma to gather the eggs under Selma, Grandma's oldest hen—the one that was the best layer.

Selma didn't like Jenny and wouldn't get off her nest when the young girl came to gather the eggs each day. Selma gave her eggs only to Grandma, who would look Selma directly in the eyes and say, "Move!"

When Jenny shouted "Move!" to Selma, the hen just glared back defiantly. If Jenny tried sticking her hand under Selma to steal the eggs, she got her hand pecked.

Jenny had tried to argue her way out of the chicken chores by suggesting that Audrey could do a better job and make Selma mind, but Grandma would hear none of her complaints.

"Do what you're told," was Grandma's standard reply. "The challenge will do you good. You may learn something about chicken negotiations by the end of the summer."

Each day, Jenny grew a bit more frustrated as she continued her battle with Selma. This morning, she was determined. She decided to bribe Selma with a special treat. A dish full of Grandma's rice might do the trick.

Jenny had heard Grandpa mention that birds liked the rice he put into all his sheds. They gobbled it down and never came into his sheds again. Maybe Selma would gobble the rice down and never come back to the chicken coop.

After Jenny put the chicken feed into the food tray and filled the water fountain from the well, she took her egg basket with the bowl full of rice inside and entered the chicken coop to confront Selma.

Selma glared at Jenny as she approached. Jenny held the rice out to Selma and slowly moved closer to the hen, until the rice was right under Selma's nose.

Jenny feeding Selma rice

Selma sat quietly for a minute, sniffing at the rice in the bowl, and then she started pecking at it. After she had eaten several grains, Jenny moved the bowl a few inches from Selma's nose. Selma got up and stretched her neck to get the rice.

She likes it, Jenny thought with a big grin on her face. *This will work.*

Jenny gradually moved the bowl farther away from Selma along the nesting ledge. Selma's neck wasn't long enough to reach the rice, so Selma stepped out of her nest to follow the bowl. Then Jenny spilled the rice on the chicken coop floor, and Selma jumped down off the nesting ledge to get the rice scattered there.

Jenny moved quickly and took the eggs out of Selma's nest. She put them into the egg basket and quickly gathered the rest of the eggs, while Selma ate happily off the floor. When she had finished the task, Jenny hurried to the house. She couldn't wait to tell Grandma how she had outsmarted Selma.

✳   ✳   ✳   ✳

"I did it, I did it!" Jenny shouted as she burst through the kitchen door.

"Did what, child?"

Grandma appeared startled as she looked up from mixing her bread dough.

"I got Selma's eggs—all by myself."

"Well ..." Grandma smiled. "I told you that you'd figure it out."

"I fed her some of your rice. It's spilled all over the chicken coop floor, and Selma is busy eating right now."

Grandma dropped her mixing spoon in horror.

"How much rice did you feed her?"

"A bowlful."

"Good Lord, child! You'll kill my chicken."

Grandma rushed out the kitchen door shouting to Jenny, "Get the broom and dustpan."

Jenny set down the egg basket, grabbed the broom and dustpan, and ran after Grandma, who was already halfway to the chicken coop. Jenny had never seen Grandma move so fast.

"What's wrong, Grandma?" Jenny asked when she caught up. "Grandpa said the birds really liked his rice, and they never returned."

"Birds can't eat too much rice or they could die," Grandma replied, half out of breath, as she ran toward the chicken coop.

"Why?" Jenny asked, running next to Grandma.

"Because when they drink water after they eat all that rice, it swells up inside their stomach and could kill them or make them sick."

Jenny realized she had made a horrible mistake.

"I'm sorry," she moaned.

When they reached the chicken coop, Grandma put her arms around Jenny.

"It's all right," Grandma said. "You didn't mean to hurt Selma, I'm sure."

Selma was busy eating rice when they entered the coop.

"Shoo, shoo!" Grandma shouted and chased Selma out of the coop. Then she swept up the rest of the rice from the floor.

Jenny stood and watched with a sad face. She didn't like Selma, but she hadn't wanted to kill her, either.

When the cleaning was done, Grandma instructed Jenny to take the dirty rice to the burning barrel. Grandma walked slowly back to the house.

Jenny came running up beside Grandma and took her hand.

"I'm sorry, Grandma; I didn't mean to hurt your favorite hen."

"I know that. I think Selma will be okay. We'll know by tomorrow. There was quite a bit of the rice left on the floor, and Selma's a tough old bird, so she'll probably be okay."

Grandma smiled as she patted Jenny on the back.

∗   ∗   ∗   ∗

Sheriff Whippert entered the yard right after lunch. He honked his horn until the Haskells came out of the house.

His appearance was no surprise, since Audrey had mentioned to Grandpa at breakfast that the children had something to tell the sheriff. Grandpa had called the lawman as soon as he had time.

Audrey started the confession.

"We went riding with the Cavetts yesterday," she said, "down by the James River."

"And …"

The sheriff tried to move the story along. He had other business to attend to.

Denny took over the story.

"We discovered an old abandoned cabin next to the river, and—"

"We saw a man leave the cabin on a motorcycle when we were hiding in the weeds," Jenny interrupted.

Sheriff Whippert seemed a bit upset.

"What were you kids doing spying on someone, anyway? That's private property up there," he said.

"I'm sure they didn't mean any harm," Grandpa defended the children. "Kids will be kids, Andy."

The sheriff frowned.

"We didn't mean any harm," Ty said with big, sorrowful eyes.

Ty looked so woeful that the sheriff had to laugh.

"Go on," Sheriff Whippert said. "What happened?"

"Not much," Audrey said, trying to sound nonchalant. "We went inside the cabin and snooped into his duffel bag when he was gone and found a gun. Maybe he's the one killing the deer?"

"I doubt it," Sheriff Whippert said firmly. "You kids shouldn't be snooping around in other people's things. Besides, most of us around here have a gun or two. Your grandpa has a couple guns, don't you, Josh?"

"Yes, but I don't keep them hidden in duffel bags, and I don't sneak around in old, abandoned cabins," Grandpa said. "I think the kids have a legitimate clue here. Maybe this guy does have something to do with the deer killings. It wouldn't hurt you to check it out. It's been two months now that this has been going on, and you haven't solved the mystery—not that I've heard, anyway."

"We're investigating all the angles, Josh. Give me a break here."

"I'm not going to tell you your job, Andy, but it wouldn't hurt you to check out some of the clues the kids found to see if you can stop these senseless killings."

"I'll work on it, Josh," the sheriff said. "In the meantime, you keep those kids away from that cabin. If that guy is killing deer, he probably wouldn't mind shooting a few kids, either."

Ty's eyes grew wide with fright. Grandpa put his arm around the young boy and assured the sheriff that his grandchildren would not be bothering the guy in the cabin again.

With that said, Sheriff Whippert left in a huff.

After the car was out of sight, Grandpa turned to the children.

"You heard the sheriff. I don't want any of you going up to that cabin again. Do you all hear me?"

"Yes, Grandpa," the children responded in unison. They were very happy that Grandpa had defended them against the sheriff's rebuke.

"Now, let's go fishing," Grandpa said.

He smiled and headed for the pickup.

*   *   *   *

The first thing Jenny did the next morning was race out to the chicken coop to check on Selma. When she entered the coop and saw Selma sitting defiantly on her nest, Jenny started jumping up and down clapping her hands and yelling at the top of her voice. The noise frightened Selma so much that she jumped out of her nest and ran out of the coop.

Jenny quickly took Selma's eggs and headed back to the house.

"Guess what?" Jenny shouted as she entered the kitchen door where the rest of the Haskells were having breakfast. "Selma is alive, and I also figured out a way to get her eggs. She doesn't like wild, crazy jumping and yelling, so she leaves her nest."

"I don't blame her," Grandpa said. "I don't like wild, crazy jumping and yelling, either. Now, sit down and eat."

CHAPTER 13

▼

JULY FOURTH
CELEBRATION

"All we do is work, work, work!" Jenny complained to Grandma while wiping the supper dishes. "When are we going to have some fun?"

"We'll have lots of things to do tomorrow," Grandma assured her. "There are always plenty of activities at the Fourth celebration in Golva."

"I'll bet!" Jenny said sarcastically. "What could that one-horse town do that would be fun?"

"Well, for starters, we're going to ride to town in the old buggy with Bessie pulling it, so we can be in the parade. Grandpa and I always ride the old buggy in the parade."

Jenny's eyes lit up. "Can I drive, too?"

"Sure, you can all learn to drive the horse and buggy—it's fun."

*   *   *   *

"I'm first because I'm the oldest," Audrey declared when Grandpa asked who would like to take the reins and guide Bessie.

The Haskell family in the buggy

"Whoa, Bessie," Grandpa said.

Bessie stopped and gave Grandpa a curious look. Then Grandma moved to the backseat of the buggy, and Audrey moved up beside Grandpa.

Grandpa showed her how to hold the reins properly.

"Now there's about four commands to learn," he told her. "'Giddyup' means start. Do that while you gently hit the reins on Bessie's rump. 'Whoa' means stop. Pull the reins tight when you say that. When you want to go left, tug on the left rein, and when you want to go right, tug on the right rein. Let's try it—I'll be right here to help."

Audrey gently slapped the reins on Bessie's rump and said, "Giddyup."

They were off at a brisk walk.

"This is great, Grandpa," Audrey gushed. "How can we go faster?"

"Well, Bessie doesn't go much faster, but she might run a bit if you slapped the reins on her rump a little harder and shouted 'giddyup.'"

Bessie took off on a slow run when Audrey gave her second command. The buggy hit a bump in the road, and all the passengers bounced up from their seat.

They all laughed.

"That was cool," Denny said. "I can't wait for my turn. I'm going to make Bessie run fast."

"No, you're not!" Grandma said firmly. "We're going plenty fast right now. I don't want anyone to bounce out of this buggy on their head."

The children took turns; each one got to drive about half a mile. Ty was driving when they entered the town of Golva.

"I'll take over now," Grandpa said. "Too many people and cars here—Bessie might get spooked and bolt."

Grandpa drove the buggy to the fairgrounds and got in line at the end of the parade. Since they were early, Grandpa let the children walk around and look at the other parade entries. There were old cars, old tractors, decorated floats, and lots of cars full of politicians running for office. There was also a display of new farm machinery and cars that the local dealers wanted to show off.

The parade started at 10:00 AM. The Haskells led the horse entries at the end of the parade. The horses were always at the end of a parade, because sometimes they went to the bathroom during the parade, and the other floats or people on foot didn't want to walk through horse do-do.

Grandma had purchased several bags of individually wrapped candy for the children to throw to spectators along the parade route. While Audrey, Denny, and Jenny threw candy, Ty ate his share. He figured that he wouldn't be in the audience to catch any candy, so he'd better eat the ones he had.

*   *   *   *

When the parade ended, everyone gathered on Main Street, and the activities began.

There were footraces for all ages, beginning with four-year-olds. Ty ran with the boys aged seven. He didn't win, but he got a Snickers candy bar for trying—as did everyone who ran.

Jenny came in first for her race, Audrey took third, and Denny took second—Randy beat him.

The boys were happy with their winnings, but not everyone watching was happy.

Al Meyer, the thirteen-year-old town bully, shouted "Dumb Indian!" when Randy won the race and walked between two buildings on Main Street.

Randy was not one to take insults lightly, so he walked up to Al, gave him a shove, and said, "Sissy white guy—go run with the girls."

Al shoved Randy back, and the fight was on. Denny took Randy's side and started swinging. Since he'd never been in a fight, he wasn't very good at it. Al screamed in pain as Randy grabbed his bright, carrot red hair and pulled some of it out. Then three of Al's friends came to his rescue, and soon Randy and Denny were outnumbered. Two of Al's friends were holding Randy while Al punched him. Denny was busy trying to contain the smallest of the Golva bullies.

Jenny and Missy noticed the skirmish that was going on in the alley between two Main Street buildings. They went to see what was happening. When they saw that Randy and Denny were in trouble, they joined the fight, jumping on the backs of Al and one of his bully friends and hitting them on their heads. The crowd that was gathering cheered the girls on.

Jenny bit Al's arm so he would release Randy. Al screamed. The blood from the bite smeared on her jacket as Al released Randy to get Jenny off his back.

A city policeman came running when he heard someone yelling, "Fight, fight!"

The policeman and several other adults broke up the fight and told the children to get cleaned up.

"If I catch you kids fighting again, I'll haul you off to jail," the policeman threatened.

Randy and Denny dusted themselves off. Except for the bloody nose Randy had and Denny's battered eye, which would probably turn black, they seemed no worse for the ordeal.

"I hope Grandma didn't see the fight," Denny said. He knew she would be angry.

"Nah," Randy assured him, "they're busy watching the watermelon eating contest inside the community building. We're safe."

Then Randy looked at Jenny and Missy, all dirty and disheveled.

"Thanks," he said with a smile. "You girls got guts. We couldn't have done it without you."

"You're welcome," Jenny said, dusting off her blood-smeared jacket. "It was a blast!"

Missy didn't say a word; she felt very uncomfortable brawling in the streets, but she wasn't going to let anyone call her brother names. When kids called her names, Randy always stuck up for her—now she'd paid him back.

*   *   *   *

After the fight, Randy and Denny entered the three-legged race. They started off fast and were way ahead of the other boys when Denny slipped and fell. Randy picked him up and tried to get back into the race, but it was too late. Another pair had passed them and crossed the finish line first. Randy and Denny came in second.

"You klutz," Randy chided Denny. "I tripped over your big feet."

"My feet aren't any bigger than yours!" Denny shot back.

Randy started to laugh.

"You look great with that puffy eye. You're going to have quite a shiner there, buddy."

Denny grinned. He had never had a real black eye before. He was proud of the defense he had put up for his friend. It was a good day.

The boys put their arms around each other and walked away from the race, happy to have taken second place.

*   *   *   *

The community picnic in the city park was great fun. Each family brought their own food, and the local merchants supplied drinks and ice cream. The Haskells and Cavetts sat at the same table. Denny tried to hide his face from Grandma, but she finally noticed.

Grandma looked shocked. "Good Lord, child, what happened to your eye?" she asked.

"He had a fight," Jenny said proudly. "We were all in it. The other kids started it. They called Randy a dumb Indian."

Emma Cavett gave Randy a stern look and said, "You've been called worse, Randy. You know better than to react to such talk."

Grandpa and Elmer were trying hard to keep from laughing.

"Oh well, Emma," Grandpa said, "boys will be boys."

"It looks like girls will be boys in this bunch," Grandma said with disgust. "It's bad enough that our boys are ruffians, but you girls should be ladies, and ladies don't brawl in the streets."

Elmer tried to calm her down.

"Let them be, Abby," he said. "They were only trying to help Randy. It's noble to help out a friend. They did a good thing."

"Well, I'm not in favor of *any* fighting for *any* reason," Grandma said, "but I guess they've got to learn to defend themselves. Those other children should not have been calling Randy names. That's disgraceful."

*   *   *   *

After the picnic, all the children went looking for ways to spend their money. Grandma had given them their weekly allowances, so along with the money they won for the races, they were rich.

"Let's go play some carnival games and go on some rides," Randy suggested.

"I'd rather buy a cowgirl hat at the souvenir stand," Audrey announced as she headed for the stand.

"Wait for me," Ty yelled, running after her. "I want a hat too."

Missy, Jenny, Randy, and Denny walked on to the carnival, where they picked some ducks out of a swimming tank and won a few small prizes. Randy threw some balls at a target and won a tiny teddy bear, which he gave to Missy. Denny tossed rings onto canes and won a key chain.

"What you going to do with that key chain?" Randy teased. "You don't have a key for anything."

"I'll save it until I do," Denny assured him.

After several rides on the tilt-a-whirl and the swings, the four fighters were broke, so they sat on a bench in the shade and talked.

"What should we do now?" Missy asked.

"I'm hot and tired," Jenny complained. "I think I'll go back to the park and rest in the shade of the trees until the free entertainment starts at three."

"That sounds like a good plan," Missy said, following Jenny toward the park.

When the girls were out of earshot, Randy turned to Denny.

"You know, we should go back to the cabin sometime and see if we can find some more clues," Randy said.

"Grandpa said we can't go back there, or we'll be in big trouble."

"I dare you."

"What if we get shot at?" Denny asked.

"Chicken!"

"I'm no chicken. I just don't want to get into trouble."

"No one will find out," Randy said. "We'll go by ourselves and won't take Audrey, so we don't have to tell the sheriff."

"How're we going to do that?"

Randy had a plan. "Why don't you and Jenny ask if you can sleep over at our place some night? We'll tell our grandparents that we want to sleep outside in our tent, then we'll sneak away at night and spy on the guy in the cabin."

Denny's eyes lit up.

"Awesome! We'll make it a secret mission, and no one will ever know."

"Yeah. Let's go tell Missy and Jenny, but not Audrey and Ty—they'll squeal on us."

The boys raced to the park and found the two girls resting in the shade of a big tree, eating some more of the free ice cream.

Randy relayed the plan to the girls, and they approved. Then they plotted their strategy while eating ice cream on a beautiful Fourth of July afternoon.

*   *   *   *

On the buggy ride home, the children were grumbling that they didn't get to stay for the evening fireworks.

"We've got chores to do at home," Grandma explained. "The animals can't feed themselves, you know."

"We can see the fireworks from the hayloft in the barn," Grandpa assured the children. "When it gets dark, we'll grab some blankets, open the loft doors, and watch the show."

They celebrated the end of a perfect holiday when the stars came out. The whole family cuddled together and watched the beautiful display of fireworks from a distance.

CHAPTER 14

▼

A FRIGHTENING
EXPERIENCE

"Grandma, can Denny and I do something special on our birthday this weekend?" Jenny asked politely after she'd finished her chores on Tuesday morning.

"What would you like to do?"

"Could we stay overnight with Missy and Randy? They said they would like us to do that sometime."

"We'll see," Grandma replied. "I'll have to call Emma and make sure it's all right with her. We could have ice cream and cake here on Saturday afternoon, and then you could go home with the Cavetts after that and stay overnight. The Cavetts could bring you back on Sunday morning in time for church."

Jenny didn't care if they missed church, but she figured she'd better agree to Grandma's suggestions or risk the possibility of getting all their plans nixed.

"Thanks, Grandma," she said as she ran out of the house to tell Denny.

✳   ✳   ✳   ✳

It seemed that Saturday would never come. After Grandma had approved the overnight stay with Emma, Denny and Jenny called Randy and Missy and plotted and planned what they would do on Saturday night.

The day finally arrived, and the twins had their birthday party Saturday afternoon. Besides the Cavetts, Grandma had invited Pastor Bender and his wife, Irene.

The children and some of the adults played softball and Anti-I-Over until they were exhausted. Later, they sat in the shade of the big ash tree in the backyard and had grilled hamburgers, potato salad, baked beans, and Grandpa's homemade ice cream with their birthday cake.

The twins got to open their gifts after the party. In the excitement, they almost forgot about their overnight plans.

Jenny got a pair of designer jeans from Grandma and Grandpa. She had looked at the jeans in the preteen store in Aberdeen a few weeks ago, but she couldn't afford to buy them. After Grandpa and the children were in the car, Grandma went back into the mall and purchased the jeans, using the excuse that she had forgotten one of her packages in JCPenny. Jenny thanked her grandparents profusely, saying that the gift was exactly what she wanted.

Jenny also got a musical jewelry box from the Cavetts and a silver cross from the Benders. After Jenny had opened her last gift, Grandma went into the bedroom and brought out a box she had been saving.

"Here's something your parents sent from Central America last week for your birthday," she told the twins. "I've been saving this package for today."

The twins quickly opened their package and found two T-shirts. The one that was bright yellow with an Aztec Indian sundial design had Jenny's name printed on the back. The other one was turquoise with an Indian pony design and had Denny's name on the back. The twins were delighted with the T-shirts and put them on immediately.

Denny also got a new Nintendo game from Grandma and Grandpa, a flashlight he could wear around his neck from the Cavetts, and a book of Bible stories from the Benders. He was delighted with the gifts and beamed as he opened each one.

After saying "thank you" to everyone, the twins put their things in their rooms and packed their overnight suitcases. Then they sat and waited for the adults to get done talking, so they could go home with Missy and Randy to ride the ponies.

*   *   *   *

"We'll be fine, Grandma, don't worry," Randy assured his grandmother as the children crawled into the small tents they had set up earlier. It was getting dark outside, and the four friends were anxious to start their spying adventure.

"Now, you four get to sleep. I don't want you up all night talking. You won't be able to get up for church in the morning," Grandma Emma said sternly.

"We won't talk long," Missy promised. "We just want to visit a little longer."

"Good night, then. Sleep tight and don't let the bedbugs bite," Grandma Emma teased as she walked toward the house.

Randy breathed a sigh of relief.

"Good—she's gone," he said. "I thought she would never leave. We'll wait until she and Grandpa get to sleep, then we'll take off. I can hardly wait. I'll bet we find some new, exciting clues tonight."

"I just hope we don't get shot," Denny mumbled. "Maybe we ought to think this over."

"Chicken!" Randy taunted.

"Don't call me that. I'm no chicken. I just hope ... well ... I hope everything goes okay."

"It will. We need some excitement around here," Randy said with enthusiasm.

Then he yelled over to the girls' tent.

"Hey, Missy and Jenny, you girls ready to rumble?"

Missy tried to quiet Randy down.

"Shish, not so loud," she said. "Grandma and Grandpa will hear."

"Grandpa's already in bed, and Grandma will be there soon," Randy assured everyone. "As soon as the light goes off, we're out of here."

Five minutes later, the light went off, and the children headed for the barn where the ponies were waiting—still saddled up after the children's early-evening rides. The boys hadn't taken the saddles off after the rides.

"It will go faster this way," Randy had assured Denny, who had wondered if the horses would mind waiting with their saddles on.

*   *   *   *

It hadn't rained in some time, and the river was very low. The children found a narrow, shallow spot upstream from the cabin and crossed it on horseback. They tied the ponies to some trees and walked toward the cabin.

The lights were out, and the motorcycle was sitting in front of the cabin.

"Maybe we'd better wait here a minute and watch to see if there is any movement inside," Denny suggested as the children approached the cabin.

They didn't wait for long. The children grew impatient and decided to peek inside the window. They crept around the side of the cabin. Just as they were crawling up to the window, they heard a low growl.

"Grrrrrrrrrr."

They froze!

"What was that?" Randy whispered to Denny.

"It sounded like a d-dog. I don't th-think he's out here," Denny answered fearfully.

Randy tried to calm the others.

"I don't know …" he said. "Stay still. We'll see what happens."

The four spies remained motionless as a dim light went on inside the cabin.

Jenny panicked.

"Run for it!" she shouted as she took off toward where they had left the ponies.

"Wait for me, Jenny," Missy screeched in horror, running after her.

The boys lay frozen in the tall grass near the house. Just then, the front door burst open, and a man with a big black dog appeared in the moonlight.

"Who's out here?" he called.

The dog began barking and pulling at his leash.

"Stay, Blackie!" the man ordered the dog.

In the moonlight, the man spotted Jenny's cap, which had fallen off during her hasty retreat. He walked out on the path and picked it up, holding tightly to his dog's restraint.

"If he lets that dog go, we're dead meat," Randy whispered to Denny, with panic in his voice.

Denny, who was shivering with fear, began to pray silently, "Our father …"

"Stay, Blackie!" the man ordered his dog again while pulling on the dog's collar. "We'll look for evidence of intruders in the morning."

The man went back inside the cabin, pulling the dog along.

After the door closed, Randy whispered, "Let's go."

The boys ran toward the ponies in terror, as fast as their legs could carry them. The grass was very high in one spot, and Denny tripped over something.

"Aaaaahhhhh!" he screamed as he went rolling into the grass.

The boys running in terror and Denny falling

"What's wrong now, you klutz?" Randy asked as he stopped to help Denny up.

"I tripped over something."

"Where?"

Denny pointed. "Right back there a few feet."

The boys pushed the grass aside and found a deer carcass.

Randy touched the dead deer.

"This doe hasn't been dead too long," he said. "She's still warm."

Denny wrinkled his nose in disgust.

"You city kids sure are squeamish," Randy said. "Come on, let's go."

*   *   *   *

When the boys arrived where the ponies were tied, they saw Jenny holding something, with Missy trying to help.

"What you got there?" Denny asked.

"A baby deer," Missy answered. "We found it wandering around. It was lost and very frightened."

"I'll bet this baby belongs to that dead doe Denny tripped over back there," Randy said.

Jenny and Missy looked shocked and were unable to speak for a few moments.

Jenny broke the silence. "Oh no," she muttered with sympathy. "What should we do with this fawn? We can't leave it here. Some wolves or other predators will eat it."

"We'll take it home," Randy suggested. "We can decide what to do with it when we get there."

Denny said, "Let's get out of here. There may be deer killers lurking in the grass somewhere."

He quickly climbed onto Jasper.

Jenny got up on Blossom, and then Randy handed her the fawn.

Missy crawled into her saddle on Blossom, Randy got into his saddle on Jasper, and the four spies plus the little fawn headed for home.

*   *   *   *

The children's fears calmed a bit as they rode home in the moonlight. They discussed the loss of Jenny's hat but decided not to worry, because the man in the cabin didn't know that the hat belonged to Jenny.

The baby deer had stopped struggling and had fallen asleep from exhaustion.

"What are we going to do with this baby?" Jenny questioned.

Missy answered.

"We'll have to feed him some milk with a bottle like we do with lambs when they lose their mothers," she said.

"Will they drink cow's milk?" Jenny asked.

"I suppose. Baby lambs drink cow's milk when there is nothing else to drink," Missy said.

"Do you suppose he's hungry?"

"Maybe. We'll see when we get home."

*   *   *   *

The boys put the ponies into the barn, fed them, and unsaddled them, while the girls got the fawn ready for bed in their tent.

When the boys came to the girls' tent, they all discussed what to do with the fawn.

"I'll sneak into the house and get a bottle full of milk," Missy offered. "I know where the bottles are kept. I fed our lambs bottles this spring."

"You'll have to be very quiet, or you'll wake your grandparents," Denny warned.

"I can be very quiet when I want to be. Besides, Grandma and Grandpa are both hard of hearing. They'll never wake up."

After a few minutes, Missy was back with a bottle of warm cow's milk. The fawn didn't seem to be interested in drinking at first, but when Missy squirted some of the milk in his mouth and he swallowed it, he took the nipple and drank greedily.

After the fawn was fed and had settled down, the children went to sleep, exhausted from their frightening adventure.

CHAPTER 15

▼

LIAR, LIAR, PANTS ON FIRE!

"Gross!" Jenny said with disgust as she sat up on the air mattress and stared at the baby deer.

"What's wrong?" Missy asked, turning over on the mattress.

"He's going potty on our sleeping bag!"

Missy sat up to look.

"That's not a he—it's a she. Look again, Jenny."

"Whatever. It's still gross. What will we tell your grandmother?"

"We'll have to tell her that you wet the bed," Missy said seriously.

"No way!"

"We can't tell her a deer wet the bed. She'd want to know where the deer came from, and we'd blow our whole story."

A frown covered Jenny's face. *How embarrassing—what will Grandma Emma think!*

"I haven't wet the bed since I was two," Jenny protested.

Missy gave Jenny a stern look.

Jenny paused a moment to think. She knew Missy was right. Finally, she relented.

"If we must, we must, but maybe we could just hang the sleeping bag out to dry and your grandma won't notice."

"We could try, but Grandma is pretty good at smelling things. She'll smell it on the sleeping bag when she comes to put it away."

"I'll be gone by then, so you can tell her whatever you want," Jenny said defiantly as she rolled up the sleeping bag.

"Let's tell the boys what happened," Missy suggested after the bag was hanging on the clothesline. "We all need to decide what to do with the fawn before Grandma and Grandpa find it."

✳   ✳   ✳   ✳

The four spies were sitting in the boys' tent deciding where to put the fawn when they heard Grandma call, "Breakfast's ready in ten minutes. Get up, you sleepyheads."

"Let's sneak the fawn down to the barn for now, until we can decide what to do with her," Randy suggested.

"What if Grandma and Grandpa see us?" Missy asked worriedly.

Denny said, "Randy can carry the fawn, and the rest of us will form a circle around him and walk really close."

"Good plan," Jenny agreed as she stood up. "Let's go."

The four went to the girls' tent, where the fawn was sleeping on the air mattress.

"Look out," Jenny warned as she entered the tent. "She's done another job on the grass in the corner."

"Pee-eww." Denny held his nose.

"You city kids are sure finicky," Missy muttered as Randy picked up the fawn.

The group huddled together and moved the fawn slowly to the barn.

Grandpa Elmer, who was watching the procedure out of the kitchen window, remarked to Grandma Emma, "What are those kids up to? Looks like they are taking something to the barn."

"Who knows? Those four have some great imaginations. They probably are moving a rock or other precious possession."

"We'll have to ask them when they get in for breakfast," Grandpa Elmer said as he sat down to eat.

The children entered the house quietly and washed their hands and faces in the entrance bathroom. Then they sat down silently and began helping themselves to Grandma Emma's scrambled eggs and pancakes.

"What did you kids move to the barn?" Grandpa Elmer asked as he sipped his coffee.

"Nothing," Denny replied quickly, not looking up from his plate.

"Randy?" Grandpa questioned.

Randy lied without blinking an eye.

"We found some fresh-cut hay yesterday and put it into the tents to sleep on last night," he said, "and we thought we'd feed it to the ponies this morning."

"Oh, yeah, that," Denny said, joining the lying.

"It was nice of you to think of the horses," Grandma Emma said sweetly.

Grandpa Elmer gave Randy and Denny a suspicious look, frowned, and continued eating his breakfast.

✳   ✳   ✳   ✳

The boys quickly ate and then went out to the barn, making the excuse that they had to take care of the horses. The girls offered to do the breakfast dishes while the grandparents read the Sunday morning paper.

"Those kids are acting strange," Grandpa Elmer said as he picked up the sports section. "I'll have to see what's up in the barn after I'm done here."

"They may be acting strange, but it's nice to see them so helpful," Grandma Emma commented as she grabbed the life-style portion of the paper and began reading.

✳   ✳   ✳   ✳

"He's onto us," Randy said when they were safely inside the barn. "We're going to have to get this fawn out of here, or he'll eventually find it and we'll have to tell him where we got it."

"We could take it to our place," Denny volunteered.

"How?"

"Horseback."

"When?"

"Now."

"We're going to church in an hour," Randy reminded Denny. "We need to get ready."

"Let's say that I forgot my good shoes at home and we need to ride over there quickly and get them."

"That won't work. My grandma will call your grandma, and she'll bring the shoes to church so you can put them on."

"I never thought about that," Denny said. "All this lying gets kind of mixed up after a while. Maybe we should tell the truth."

Randy shook his head.

"We'll really get busted then. We weren't supposed to go near the cabin. We can hide the fawn in our chicken coop until after dinner, and then Missy and I will bring her over to your place on horseback."

"Good plan. We can hide her in the rabbit house with Cottontail—he won't mind," Denny offered. "Grandma and Grandpa don't check the rabbit anymore. But we'll have to tell Audrey and Ty, or they'll squeal on us."

"You swear them to secrecy—using the Peanut Butter Club pledge," Randy said.

"Good idea. Let's go before your grandpa comes out."

The boys moved the fawn to the chicken coop and went back to the house to dress for church.

*   *   *   *

"After they got home from church and had lunch, the children had a club meeting in Cottontail's house.

"We've got a secret to tell you," Jenny announced as soon as they were all seated, "but you mustn't tell anyone. Promise?"

"We promise," Audrey and Ty responded in unison.

"Repeat the Peanut Butter Club pledge and hope to die if you tell," Denny said as he put his fist over his heart.

Audrey and Ty repeated the pledge together, then sat patiently waiting for the twins to reveal their secret.

"Okay, here's the scoop," Jenny began. "We've got a baby deer over at the Cavetts, and—"

Audrey interrupted.

"A baby deer? Where'd you get it from?"

"That's a long story," Denny said, then he proceeded to tell the whole story to his cousins, who were mesmerized by his tale.

"Wow," Ty whispered in awe when Denny had finished. "I can't wait to see the fawn."

Denny told his cousins, "Missy and Randy are going to be here this afternoon with the fawn, and we'll have to hide it for a while. We thought this rabbit house would be a good place."

"That fawn can't live in this little house," Audrey protested. "She'll have to have a place to run and play."

"We know," Jenny said. "Grandma and Grandpa don't come out here, so she can play inside the fence."

"That will only work for a while," Audrey said. "When she grows bigger, she'll jump over the fence."

"Do you have a better plan?" Jenny asked sarcastically.

"Well, no," Audrey admitted. "I guess that will have to do for now."

"Let's go wait for Missy and Randy at the bridge," Denny said, and he got up to leave.

*   *   *   *

Missy and Randy came riding down the road at 2:00 PM. The children ran to meet them. Missy had covered the baby deer with a blanket. She handed the fawn—blanket and all—to Audrey, who was anxious to hold the baby.

"Oh look," Audrey cooed as she removed some of the blanket and showed Ty the fawn. "Isn't she beautiful? What did you name her?"

"Hope," Missy answered.

"Hope?"

"Yes," Missy replied. "We *hope* the sheriff will find her mother's killer, and we *hope* that we don't get caught with this fawn."

The six friends laughed nervously at Missy's joke, but they all knew that if they got caught, they'd be in big trouble.

CHAPTER 16

▼

BUSTED!

"All four of you wake up and get down here on the double!"

Grandpa Josh bellowed for his grandchildren at the foot of the stairs on Monday morning.

The children were startled to hear Grandpa's voice; Grandma was the one who always woke them up in the morning if they overslept. They hurriedly dressed and came downstairs.

Grandpa sat them all down on the living room couch and started asking questions, as Grandma watched nearby.

"Why did the sheriff call early this morning and say he was coming out to see all of us? And why is there a fawn in the rabbit fence?"

The children looked stunned. No one wanted to talk. No one knew what to say.

"Maybe we'll start with you, Denny," Grandpa said. "No lies now. I need some answers before the sheriff gets here."

Denny knew his lies had caught up with him, so he decided to tell Grandpa the truth. As Denny told the story, with embellishments from Jenny, Grandpa listened patiently—never saying a word—but grew visibly angrier with each detail.

When Denny was done, he hung his head in shame, waiting for Grandpa to explode.

"What were you thinking?" Grandpa said with his teeth clenched to control his anger. "I told you never to go back to that cabin."

"Well ... we—" Denny muttered.

"They were only trying to help solve the deer killings," Audrey interrupted, trying to defend the twins. "They—"

"You stay out of this, Audrey," Grandpa said sternly. "Let Denny and Jenny explain their behavior."

"I don't know what we were thinking," Jenny said submissively, not looking at Grandpa. "I'm sorry."

"You could have both been hurt," Grandma said. "Your parents would be furious if you got hurt."

Then Grandpa's voice mellowed a bit.

"You should be sorry," he said. "Both of you will explain this whole sorry mess to the sheriff and hope he doesn't take any legal action against you for trespassing on private property."

After a brief pause, Grandpa added, "We'll talk about this some more after we've talked to the sheriff."

*   *   *   *

The children ate their breakfast in silence, then hurried out to check on Hope and Cottontail.

"Don't forget your chores," Grandma called after them as they left.

When the children were far enough away from the house that their grandparents couldn't hear them, Audrey looked at Denny and Jenny.

"See what you two have gotten us into? We'll probably be confined to the farm for the rest of our stay here."

"We were only trying to help," Denny shot back.

"Yeah," Jenny agreed. "And besides, we couldn't leave the little fawn alone; some wolf would have eaten her."

"Well, you did have enough sense to bring the poor little orphan home. I'll give you credit for that," Audrey said.

The children fed the fawn and bunny, and played with the kittens for a while.

"We'd better go do our chores now," Audrey suggested, "or we'll have Grandma mad at us, too."

As they came around the corner of the barn, the sheriff drove into the yard. There was someone else in the car with him.

"That's the man from the cabin," Denny whispered to Audrey.

"I know. Remember, I saw him drive away the first time we were there?"

"Let's hide," Jenny said with fear in her voice.

"No!" Denny replied emphatically, looking at his sister. "It's time to come clean."

The children saw the sheriff's car go up the driveway and stop in front of the porch where Grandma and Grandpa were resting.

The sheriff and the tall stranger got out of the car to greet the grandparents.

"This is special agent Fletcher Brown Bear," Sheriff Whippert told Josh and Abby as the Haskells walked down the porch steps. "He's here investigating the deer shootings for the federal government."

The children looked shocked and stood with their mouths slightly open as they peeked around the corner of the barn and listened to the sheriff's introduction of Brown Bear.

"It's time to go up to the house and face the music," Audrey said as she started toward the house. The rest followed.

Grandpa and the agent shook hands. Then Grandpa introduced himself and Grandma. The children gathered around their grandparents while the adults talked.

Grandpa introduced the grandchildren to Agent Brown Bear. The agent was tall and had a long black braid hanging down his back. His face had the features of a Native American.

Although the children were shocked to learn they had spied on a government agent, they each said a polite "hello" as they were introduced.

"Fletcher tells me he had visitors on Saturday night," Sheriff Whippert said. He looked at the children as he spoke in a firm voice. "Do you know anything about this?"

"W-well ... I-I ..." Denny stuttered.

"Does this cap belong to anyone here?" the agent asked as he held out Jenny's cap and looked directly at her.

Agent Brown Bear with Jenny's cap

Jenny knew she'd been busted. She'd heard about DNA tests. "It's mine," she said softly, looking down at the ground.

The sheriff was calm as he spoke.

"You children were told not to go back to the cabin, but you did anyway. You are interfering with an ongoing investigation. I could arrest you for that."

"Audrey and I weren't there," Ty burst out. "We didn't do anything."

"I know," the sheriff answered. "Randy and Missy Cavett were the other two snoopers. We've already talked to them."

"We're sorry," Denny said regretfully. "We were only trying to help."

Tears welled up in Denny's eyes, and Jenny began sobbing as she clung to Grandma.

Agent Brown Bear felt sorry for the children.

"You children could have been hurt," the agent said softly. "My dog is trained to attack. If I had let him go, he would have hurt you."

"I'm sorry," Denny said again, not knowing what else to say.

"You must stay away from the cabin," Agent Brown Bear said sternly. "We appreciate the clues you've given us, and we are investigating them, but you must never come back to the cabin."

"W-we won't. We promise," the twins said in unison.

Sheriff Whippert spoke. "We'll let it go this time. If I catch you kids snooping around again, I'll have to arrest you for trespassing."

"They'll never be back there again," Grandpa promised. "They will be grounded for the rest of their stay here."

Jenny's eyes widened, and her mouth dropped opened. She was about to complain, when Grandma put both her hands around Jenny's face and looked into her eyes.

"You'd better be quiet unless you want some additional punishment," Grandma told Jenny.

Jenny's mouth closed, and she dropped her head. She knew that anything she said at that moment would only make matters worse.

"Since Agent Brown Bear is working undercover, this must all be kept secret," the sheriff said. "You must not breathe a word of this to anyone. Understand?"

Sheriff Whippert gave each of the children a stern look. They nodded their heads in agreement.

Grandpa shook hands with the sheriff and agent, then the men got into their car, said good-bye, and drove away.

The Haskell family stood in silence for a moment.

"Go do your chores," Grandma said softly. "We'll talk about this at lunchtime."

*   *   *   *

The children did all their chores and then cleaned up their rooms. They thought that doing something extra might earn them some brownie points.

At lunchtime, the grandchildren ate the green beans with cheese sauce without a word of complaint. They didn't need Grandma Abby mad at them, too.

"Grandpa and I have decided on some appropriate punishment for Denny and Jenny," Grandma announced after she filled her plate with food. "They will not be given any allowance or be permitted to leave the farm for one week. After that, they will be allowed to go with Grandpa and me for supervised activities.

"Since Audrey and Ty weren't involved in the spying—but they were part of the cover-up—they will only lose their allowance this week. You will all be responsible for taking care of the fawn until you go home, then Grandpa and I will call the zoo in Aberdeen and see if they will take the fawn."

"But ... Hope—" Audrey began.

"No buts! Our decision is final," Grandma said firmly. "The fawn will never be able to survive in the wilderness after being confined as a baby, so someone will have to take care of her for the rest of her life. Grandpa and I are too old, so the zoo is the only answer."

The children hung their heads and ate quietly. After clearing the table, they went outside to play. It would be a long week.

CHAPTER 17

▼

GETTING A BREAK

"I need to get away from this farm for a while or I'll go buggy," Jenny lamented as she watched Audrey feed Hope some sweet clover.

Audrey feeding the fawn

"You're grounded. Don't you remember?" Audrey asked sarcastically.

"Duh! I'd still like to go fishing or something for an afternoon. Grandma said we could go on supervised trips."

Jenny paused a moment before adding, "I'll bet Grandpa would take us fishing if Ty would ask. Ty usually gets his way. Why don't you talk to him, Audrey? He'll do anything for you."

"Sure. I'll try. Now let's go pick the peas and get them shucked. Grandma's waiting for them."

The girls walked to the garden with their plastic ice cream pails. The boys, who had been mowing behind the Quonset, came riding the mower across the yard. They were going to mow down by the river. Audrey flagged them down.

"I want to ask Ty something," she shouted over the mower's roar while motioning Denny to turn it off.

"Would you do me a favor, Ty?" Audrey asked when the noise stopped.

"Sure."

"At lunchtime, ask Grandpa to take us fishing."

"Okay."

Jenny chimed in.

"Cool!" she said. "Let's go pick peas."

*   *   *   *

Grandpa's answer was, "I suppose we could do that."

So after lunch, the grandchildren got ready while Grandpa rested in his La-Z-Boy for an hour. When he awoke, they all got into the pickup and left.

The river was lower this time, because it hadn't rained for a while. Grandpa had purchased some more poles, so they all fished together for about an hour. Grandpa and Audrey were the only two to catch any fish, and the others grew restless.

"Can I go to the beach up the river and play in the sand?" Ty asked.

"Not unless someone goes with you," Grandpa replied.

"Denny, will you come?" Ty asked politely.

Denny sighed.

"Sure, why not? I'm not catching anything anyway."

He handed his fishing pole to Grandpa and said to Ty, "Come on, squirt, let's go."

The boys wandered along the river's edge until they reached the beach area where the picnic table stood.

The river had receded since the last time they were at the beach, so there was a lot more sand to play with. Ty started building a fort with the sand and some small sticks from a nearby tree. Denny helped for a while, and then decided to rest on the picnic table.

The sun beat down on Denny until he felt very warm. He crawled under the table to get some shade.

"Hey! Look what I found!" Denny yelled from under the table.

Ty looked up from his fort building.

"What?"

"Some carrot red hair."

"What?"

"Come look," Denny said.

Ty crawled under the table with Denny. He saw a tuft of red hair caught in a wood splinter under the table.

"Yeah, it's red all right," Ty agreed. "So what?"

"Don't you remember that kid in Golva on the Fourth of July who we had a fight with? He had red hair this color."

"I didn't see him. I was with Audrey."

"Oh, yeah, you're right. I'll have to get Jenny to look at this. Come on, let's go."

"I'm not done with my fort," Ty protested.

Denny took off at a fast run back toward the fishing dock. "Wait for me!" Ty called, racing after him.

*   *   *   *

When they reached the dock, Denny told Grandpa about his discovery.

"That hair could have been there for a long time," Grandpa replied.

"We were under the table before, and I didn't see any hair. I think it's recent," Denny argued. "Can Jenny come and see?"

"No. We'll all go investigate as soon as we gather up our fishing gear. We've caught enough Northern for supper, and it's getting late. We'll have to do chores soon."

The children hurriedly loaded the fish and equipment into the back of the pickup. They hopped in themselves, along with Laddie, who was eager to go home and get out of the hot sun.

*   *   *   *

"That looks like 'Big Al's' hair, all right," Jenny said from under the table. "Could they do a DNA test on it?"

"Sure, but it wouldn't prove anything unless they have another DNA sample from Al," Grandpa replied. "His parents might not give permission for the law to do a test."

"Can blood be tested for DNA?" Jenny asked.

"Sure can."

"I know where there is some of Al's blood. I still have some drops on my jean jacket from the fight. It's been laying in back of my closet. I didn't want Grandma to see it and give me a hard time, so I've kept it hidden."

"Well, for once in you life you did something smart," Audrey said sarcastically, then smiled and patted Jenny on the back. "Good job."

"We'll call Sheriff Whippert and Agent Brown Bear when we get home," Grandpa said. "They can come and investigate if they want to."

*   *   *   *

That evening around the supper table, the Haskells discussed the latest clue to the deer killing mystery and ate a delicious meal of fresh fried fish and creamed peas.

"I love these peas, Grandma," Ty said with his mouth full of food. He was very hungry after an afternoon of fishing, running, and doing chores.

"Yes," Grandma said with a big smile on her face. "Being outdoors, working, and not getting anything else to eat can build up an appetite."

"I like all your veggies when they have cream, butter, or your cheese sauce on them," Audrey remarked.

"Me too," the twins added in unison.

"Why thank you," Grandma said politely, with a sly look on her face.

I knew they would. When there is no junk food to eat, children usually will eat what's put on the table.

"When you've cleaned your plates, you can all have some fresh raspberries," she told the kids.

"All right!" Ty shouted. "Put plenty of cream on mine."

Everyone laughed as Grandpa covered his ears.

CHAPTER 18

▼

MAD BULL

During their triweekly club meeting that Wednesday afternoon, the children discussed their latest clue.

"Do you suppose the sheriff has gone to the beach to investigate?" Denny asked.

Audrey said, "He picked up Jenny's jacket yesterday after Grandpa called. Agent Brown Bear has probably set up a stakeout near the picnic table since then. I'll bet they catch those kids soon."

"I hope so," Jenny said. "I hate that red-haired kid. He's a bully. If he goes around picking on other kids, he probably kills deer too."

Ty entered the conversation.

"Yeah, he's just plain mean, fighting with younger kids. He deserves to go to jail."

"I don't know if he'll have to go to jail—maybe just pay some fines, or be put on probation or something," Audrey said.

Just then they heard Grandma's bell ring. They hurried out of the clubhouse and raced to the house. What could Grandma want?

When they were all on the porch, Grandma said, "Something has happened at the church. Pastor Bender called and said someone went into our church and did some damage. We're all having a meeting in half an hour. Grandpa and I will be gone for a while, and you kids will have to stay home alone. Audrey is in charge. The rest of you mind her, please. We don't need any more trouble around here."

Grandma looked sternly at her grandchildren.

"Yes, Grandma," they answered.

"We'll be good," Ty promised.

"Okay then. Come on, Josh, let's go," Grandma called into the house.

"Don't forget to clean the milking stall in the barn this afternoon," Grandpa said as he came out the front door. "Old Ulla likes a clean stall and fresh hay."

✳   ✳   ✳   ✳

"Wow," Jenny said as the children walked back to the clubhouse. "I wonder what happened at the church."

"We'll know as soon as Grandma and Grandpa get home," Audrey said. "In the meantime, let's play with our pets a while, then we'll clean the stall."

After the children finished playing, Jenny and Audrey went inside the barn to clean the stall. The boys went to get the tractor-mower with the cart hooked on behind. They were going to get a bale of fresh hay from behind the Quonset.

The children were spreading the fresh hay in the clean stall and manger when they heard a frightening noise outside.

They stood frozen as a large Herford bull with long sharp horns appeared in front of the open barn door.

"Head for the hayloft!" Audrey shouted.

The children scampered up the ladder into the hayloft one at a time. Audrey was last, keeping a fearful eye on the bull as he entered the barn.

Audrey gave a sigh of relief and took a couple of deep breaths to calm herself after everyone was safe in the hayloft.

"What will we do now?" Jenny asked fearfully. "Where did that big bull come from?"

Denny shivered.

"I think he belongs to the Cavetts," he said. "Randy said they have some big, mean bulls over there."

"Oh for Pete's sake!" Audrey exclaimed. "All we need is a mad bull around here. Why did he come over here, anyway?"

"Randy likes to exaggerate," Denny assured the rest. "Maybe the bull isn't as mean as he said."

"I'm not going to try and find out," Audrey replied. "We'll just stay here until he's gone."

"How will we know when he's gone?" Ty asked.

"We'll look down the stairwell and find out, stupid," Denny answered.

"Stop that name-calling!" Audrey said firmly. "Calling people names never solved anything."

Ty stared at his cousin.

"Yeah, Denny."

After several more minutes of discussion, the children decided to peek down the stars to see if the bull was inside the barn.

"What do you see?" Jenny asked Audrey, whose head was hanging below the stairway hole.

"He's eating the hay we put into the stall."

"Oh, great," Jenny wailed, "now we have to haul more hay."

"If we ever get down from here, we can easily get more hay," Denny said.

He resigned himself to their fate.

"Let's swing on the loft rope to kill some time," he suggested.

After fifteen minutes of swinging on the rope and dropping into a big pile of hay, the children were hot and tired.

Jenny said, "Let's check the bull again."

Audrey looked down the hole and popped her head back up.

"No bull," she announced.

"Good!" Denny said.

"What's good about that?" Audrey asked. "He's probably watching for us outside."

Denny had a suggestion.

"We could peep out of the front door on this hayloft. We can see the whole front cow pasture from there."

"Good plan," Audrey agreed.

The children scampered to the door to open it a few inches so they could peek out. They saw the bull standing by the water tank—drinking water with Ulla.

"Now what?" Jenny asked.

"We'll just wait some more," Audrey said. "If we go down into the barn and try getting outside, he could see us and chase us. It's not worth taking a chance. One of us could get hurt, and I don't want to be responsible for that."

"Oh, great!" Denny complained. "We're stuck here all afternoon."

"Only until Grandma and Grandpa come home. They'll know what to do," Audrey assured them.

As the afternoon dragged on, it got hotter and hotter in the loft as the children played on the rope. They finally agreed to open the loft doors and sit on the sill, where a cool breeze was blowing.

About 4:30, they saw their grandparents' car coming over the bridge. They began jumping and shouting to get Grandma and Grandpa's attention.

*　　*　　*　　*

"Looks like Elmer brought old Herman over to visit with Ulla," Josh said to Abby as they crossed the bridge into the farmyard.

"That time of year again?" Abby asked.

"Yup. Bessie needs her yearly visit."

"Look at the barn!" Abby exclaimed. "The loft door is open, and the children are jumping and waving."

Josh stopped the car abruptly.

"What on earth …"

Abby and Josh got out of the car and entered the cow pasture fence.

"Stop, Grandma and Grandpa!" Ty shouted in horror. "The mad bull will kill you!"

Grandpa buckled over laughing. When he gained his composure, he said, "This isn't a mad bull. It's just old Herman come to visit Ulla for a few weeks. He wouldn't hurt a fly."

Grandpa with Herman the bull

Grandpa walked up to Herman and petted the bull between his horns. Then he whispered, "These city kids think you're a mean dude. What do you think of that?"

Old Herman turned his head and looked at Grandpa, then began licking Grandpa's hand.

"Come on down and meet Herman," Grandma instructed the children, who were staring in disbelief at Grandpa and the bull.

The children closed the loft doors, scampered down the stairs, and raced out to pet Herman. The old bull was delighted to have so much attention.

*   *   *   *

At supper that evening, the elder Haskells told the children about the damage that had been done to the church.

"There was nothing of much value in the church, so the vandals just splattered mud all over the pews and altar—a very nasty thing to do in God's house," Grandma said.

Everyone discussed the vandalism and asked questions, except little Ty. He seemed to be in deep thought.

"Something bothering you, Ty?" Grandpa asked.

Ty looked at Grandpa with a puzzled look.

"Why does Herman come to visit Ulla once a year?" he asked.

Grandpa looked at Grandma with a slight blush on his cheeks.

"Maybe you'd better explain it to him, Abby. I ain't much good at that."

"Well, Ty," Grandma began, "in order for a cow to give milk each year, she needs to have a calf. It takes a male animal and a female animal to produce a calf. So, Herman and Ulla get together each year and decide if Ulla will have a baby, so we can have fresh milk and other dairy products to eat."

"Oh," Ty said. After a moment in deep thought he asked, "Do you think they'll decide to have a baby this year?"

"I think so," Grandpa replied. "They've always made the right decision before."

"Good," Ty said as he shoved a spoonful of broccoli smothered with cheese sauce into his mouth. "I love dairy products," he mumbled with his mouth full of food.

"Any questions from the rest of you?" Grandma asked.

Audrey blushed and quickly said, "No."

"We studied that stuff in biology," Jenny added.

"Gross stuff!" Denny exclaimed.

He ended the discussion by putting a big forkful of mashed potatoes smothered with gravy into his mouth.

CHAPTER 19

▼

A CRIME IS SOLVED

It was Saturday night, and the children were bored. Grandpa and Grandma had gone to Golva to visit friends. They had left Audrey in charge.

After some discussion, the children decided to go for a walk before bedtime. Since they had nowhere in particular in mind, they meandered down the gravel country road toward the church they attended.

Denny and Ty were throwing gravel stones at fence posts along the way. When they hit a post, they would jump up and down excitedly.

"Got one!" Denny shouted. "That gives me ten posts to your five, Ty."

"So?" Ty answered. "I'm doing okay for a little guy."

Jenny pointed down a side road.

"Look," she said. "There are two horseback riders coming over the hill."

"It looks like Randy and Missy. Let's wave so they see us," Denny said.

"What are you guys doing?" Jenny shouted when the riders were close enough to hear.

"We're just out riding," Missy shouted back.

When the two groups met, Randy asked, "What're you guys up to?"

"We were bored, so we decided to go for a walk," Denny replied.

"Mind if we tag along?" Missy asked.

"No," Denny said, "but we don't know where we're going—just out walking."

"We could go to the church and see the damage that was done last week," Jenny suggested.

"The church has been cleaned up," Audrey informed the group. "I heard Grandma and Emma talking on the phone yesterday."

"Well, we could go anyway and have a club meeting. We haven't done that since we've been grounded," Jenny said.

Everyone but Audrey thought that Jenny's suggestion was a good one. She didn't think they should use the church for a meeting place. After some discussion, Audrey agreed, reluctantly, to go along with the rest.

When they reached their destination, the children decided to hide the horses in the old shed in back of the church where no one would see them.

*   *   *   *

"What's that?"

Missy interrupted the group as they sat in a circle in the church narthex preparing to do the club pledge.

"What's what?" Audrey asked.

"That sound. It sounds like a car coming."

Randy jumped up and ran to the window. He open it so he could hear the sound better.

"An old pickup is coming up the road," he said. "We'd better hide. We don't want anyone to catch us here. They might think we did the damage earlier this week."

The children ran helter-skelter looking for places to hide until Audrey shouted, "Stop! We need to stick together. Let's all go into the choir robe closet. It's big enough, and the robes will hide everything except our feet."

The children ran to the closet and hid among the robes.

"Stop breathing so loud," Audrey commanded. "They'll hear us."

"We're trying," Jenny answered. "Give us a break, Audrey."

*   *   *   *

The children in the closet heard the pickup park in back of the church. Then they heard voices that sounded like teenage boys talking outside beneath the window Randy had opened.

The church door opened, and the teens came inside.

A teenager with a low, mature voice said, "We'll wait in here for Al. He should be here any minute. It takes him longer because he rides his bike."

Audrey thought, *that must be Al Meyer they are waiting for— the bully with the bright red hair that we found under the picnic table.*

"Jay, is this the church you and Al trashed a few days ago?" asked a boy with a higher-pitched voice.

Aha! The one with the low voice must be Jay, Audrey thought.

"Yeah," replied Jay. "These fools always leave the door open so anyone can go inside. We were just having some fun."

"My grandparents go to this church. They were pretty upset," said the high-pitched voice.

"We didn't do any real damage—just made a mess. It was fun."

Then Jay gave an evil laugh that echoed in the church.

The spies in the closet shuddered when they heard the evil laugh.

"Sounds like a stupid thing to do," said the high-pitched voice.

"Stop your complaining, Kevin," Jay said. "You wanted to come along. I'll take you back home if you don't shut up!"

Okay, the teenager with the higher voice is called Kevin, Audrey thought.

"I'll be good," Kevin promised.

The spies in the closet heard the boys walking around in the narthex, as though they were looking for something. The children were frozen, afraid to breathe.

What if they open this closet door? Audrey thought.

Knock! Knock!

The spies in the closet jumped.

Someone was rapping at the church door.

"That must be Al," Jay said as he opened the door to greet his friend.

"Hi, Al. About time you got here. Did you bring your gun?"

Ty let out a gasp in the closet when he heard the word *gun*. Audrey quickly put her hand over Ty's mouth and held him securely.

"Did you hear that?" Kevin asked his companions.

"What now?" Jay muttered. "You are so spooked out, Kev. Just relax. Killing deer is fun. Isn't it, Al?"

"Awesome," Al replied. "I hid my gun in a culvert by our house before I left. We'll have to go back and get it when it gets dark."

"There's no rush," Jay said. "We'll drive around until it's good and dark, then we'll go down to the beach and hide out by the picnic table until those dumb deer come for a drink."

"Maybe I should go home." Kevin said.

"Chicken!" Al taunted him.

"I'm not chicken."

"Then shut up," Jay warned. "Let's get out of here. Churches give me the creeps."

*   *   *   *

"I think they're gone," Randy whispered a few moments after the sound of the pickup motor faded into the night air.

Audrey took a deep breath.

"What will we do now?" she asked.

"Let's get out of the closet," Jenny suggested.

"We've got to tell someone about those killers' plans, or more deer will die," Audrey said anxiously as she opened the closet door.

"Who?" Denny asked. "There's no phone in the church. We're two miles from home."

"The cabin where Brown Bear stays is only about four miles from here," Randy offered. "Denny and I could get there with the horses in about thirty minutes. Brown Bear seemed like a nice guy. I'll bet he'd help."

"In about thirty minutes, it will be dark outside," Audrey said. "You'll have to hurry so Brown Bear can get to the beach before the killers do."

Jenny interrupted.

"What about the rest of us?" she asked. "What can we do?"

"We'll have to walk home as quickly as we can and tell Grandpa. He'll know what to do."

"They won't be home from their visit yet," Jenny said.

"Then we'll call them. We need to hurry. It will be dark soon," Audrey said. "Let's go!"

*   *   *   *

Randy and Denny rode away from the church as fast as the horses would go. The sun had gone down, and a full moon was coming up. It would be a bright, moonlit night.

The horses got tired after the first mile, and the boys had to ride slower. They arrived at the cabin thirty-five minutes after they left the church. The horses were exhausted.

"We'd better call out and make some noise so Brown Bear doesn't send that big black dog after us," Denny suggested.

"Good idea," Randy said. He started shouting, "Help! We need help!"

Denny joined in.

No one came out of the cabin.

Denny was distressed.

"He's not home."

Randy shrugged. "Guess not. Now what do we do?"

"We wait. I don't know where else to go. The girls will talk to Grandpa, and he'll call the sheriff. I guess we just wait."

*   *   *   *

The moon was shinning brightly when Audrey and the gang got home. There were no grandparents in sight.

"They said they were going to visit Pete and Emily Miller. I'll call there," Audrey said. She went to the phone to make the call.

Pete answered the phone. He told Audrey that her grandparents left a few minutes ago and should be home soon.

"They're coming," Audrey announced to the group after she hung up the phone. "We'll just have to wait."

CHAPTER 20

▼

ACTION AT LAST!

Randy and Denny paced back and forth in front of the cabin for half and hour before Randy heard the sound of a motor in the distance.

"Someone's coming!" Randy exclaimed. "Maybe now we'll get some action."

The boys ran down the trail to meet the approaching pickup. They were waving their arms and shouting, "Stop!"

Brown Bear slammed on the brakes when he saw the boys in his headlights.

Brown Bear jumped out of the pickup.

"What are you kids doing here? I told you—"

Denny interrupted.

"We had to come. We need help," he said.

Denny rapidly told Brown Bear about what they had overheard while hiding in the church closet.

Brown Bear acted quickly.

"Hop into the pickup. I can't leave you kids here alone. It might be dangerous, with killers on the loose."

Denny froze when he opened the pickup door and saw the big black dog sitting on the seat.

"Get over, Blackie!" Brown Bear commanded. "Let the boys get in."

Blackie moved closer to his master. The boys hopped in, and the pickup sped away in the direction of the beach.

*   *   *   *

On the way to the beach, Brown Bear told the boys he had gotten the forensic reports back on the hair and the blood.

"Remember that red hair you found under the picnic table, Denny?"

Denny nodded his head.

"We matched that hair to the blood on Jenny's jacket. That was a nice piece of detective work you kids did."

Denny grinned.

"Thanks."

"We've been keeping an eye on Al and his buddies. I've been doing stakeouts at the beach every night this week. I was on my way to the beach when I ran into you boys."

"Hope we catch those poachers tonight," Randy said.

"Me too," Denny added.

*   *   *   *

When they got to the beach, Brown Bear parked the pickup on a small hill behind some bushes, so the poachers wouldn't see it when they came.

Brown Bear told the boys to stay inside the pickup so they would be safe, and then he and Blackie left.

Randy and Denny watched the agent and his dog walk down the hill and lie flat in the tall grass near the table. The boys didn't have to wait too long before they heard the noise of a vehicle motor.

The pickup parked behind some trees about a hundred yards from the beach. The three teenage boys got out of the pickup and walked toward the beach table carrying 30-30 rifles.

The three poachers separated when they got near the table. Kevin hid under the table, while Al and Jay hid behind big trees on either side of the picnic area.

✳   ✳   ✳   ✳

"It's about time you got here," Audrey shouted as she ran out of the house to meet Grandma and Grandpa, who were climbing up onto the porch.

"What's wrong, child?" Grandma asked. "You're shaking."

"We've been waiting so long for you," Audrey said, about to break down in tears. "You were supposed to be home an hour ago."

Grandma tried to explain.

"We stopped off at the Johnson's. He has been sick, so we wanted to—"

All four children jumped into the conversation and tried to tell the grandparents about their experience at the church.

"Hold on now, one at a time," Grandpa ordered.

After the children calmed down and told their story, Grandpa asked if they had called the sheriff.

"Yes, we tried, but he's not home," Jenny said in dismay.

"Abby you stay here with Ty," Grandpa instructed. "I'll take the girls to the river and see if we can find Randy and Denny. They could be in danger."

"I want to go too," Ty protested.

"No, you can't, young man. You've had enough gangbuster adventure for one night," Grandma said as she hurried Ty into the house.

*   *   *   *

"I'm tired of waiting," Randy complained. "I'm going to see what's going on. That pickup got here fifteen minutes ago. Why doesn't Brown Bear do something?"

"You'd better not leave. You heard Brown Bear—you'll ..."

Denny's words fell on deaf ears as Randy quietly got out of the pickup and crawled into the bushes.

Denny followed.

"You'll get shot," Denny whispered. "You'd better—"

"Look!"

Randy pointed toward the hill across the river.

"There's a herd of deer coming over that hill. They're coming to drink. We'd better do something, or some of those deer will get shot."

"We could honk the pickup horn and scare the deer away," Denny suggested.

"Good plan," Randy whispered as the boys crept back to the pickup and opened the door.

Everything got eerily quiet as the deer approached the water. The shooters had their guns ready. When the deer approached the river's edge, the killers jumped out of their hiding places, aimed ...

Randy lay on the pickup horn, and it blared loudly into the quiet night.

The deer scattered in every direction.

Brown Bear jumped out of the grass and shouted at the teenagers.

"Drop those rifles or I'll shoot!"

The poachers dropped their guns and ran.

Brown Bear chased Jay toward the teens' pickup. Blackie was hot on Kevin's heels, and Al was heading in the opposite direction—right toward the bushes where Denny and Randy were now hiding.

"Al's coming this way," Denny whispered to his friend. "We've got to stop him, or he'll get away."

"Let's go!" Randy yelled as he jumped out of the bushes right in front of Al. Denny was close behind.

Al stopped dead in his tracks. For a moment, he was startled; then he recognized Denny and Randy.

"It's you two punks," Al snarled. "Get out of my way!"

Randy moved quickly, grabbing Al around the waist. Denny jumped on Al's back. Together, they wrestled Al to the ground and sat on him.

"You're not so tough when you don't have your buddies around," Randy said with a grin.

*   *   *   *

Brown Bear came running up the hill after he had captured Jay and handcuffed him to the picnic table.

"Where did Al go?" the agent asked the boys when he saw them sitting in the grass.

Randy pointed to the form beneath him.

"He's down here," he said. "Denny and I caught him trying to escape."

"Good work, boys."

Brown Bear put handcuffs on Al.

"Look!"

Randy pointed.

"There are lights in the distance. Someone else is coming."

"That must be Grandpa," Denny said. "The girls must have finally gotten hold of him."

The agent put Al into the pickup bed and handcuffed him to the railing on the side of the bed.

"Let's go see what happened to Kevin. Blackie was chasing him up the road the last time I saw them," Brown Bear said.

The agent, Randy, and Denny got into the pickup and drove toward the approaching vehicle.

*   *   *   *

Grandpa and the girls saw Kevin running as fast as he could toward them as they drove down the country road toward the beach. Blackie was nipping at Kevin's heels.

"Help! Help!" Kevin cried as he approached the pickup. "This dog is going to kill me."

Grandpa and the girls jumped out of the pickup.

"Stay!" Grandpa yelled at Blackie.

The big black dog stopped in his tracks, obeying Grandpa's command. Then Grandpa took hold of Blackie's collar and held him firmly.

"Thanks," Kevin said. "That dog is mean."

Then he sat down to rest. He was shaking.

Audrey pointed at Kevin.

"That's one of the poachers," she said. "I remember his voice from when we were in the church closet."

Kevin quickly got up and started running toward the woods nearby. The girls followed him, in hot pursuit.

Audrey caught up with Kevin first and jumped on his back. Kevin kept on running, carrying Audrey on his back.

"Help!" Audrey shouted to her girlfriends. "I need help!"

Jenny and Missy heard Audrey's cry and increased their speed. They caught up with Kevin and tackled him. He went down. The girls sat on him as he screamed with pain.

"Get off me!" Kevin yelled. "I didn't do anything."

"I'll bet you didn't," Audrey said. "We'll wait for Agent Brown Bear to get here, and he'll tell us what you did."

"Good thing we had that street fight on the Fourth of July," Jenny giggled. "It taught us how to fight with the boys."

Missy grinned and said, "Sometimes a girl has got to be tough."

"You two are too much," Audrey laughed. She was pleased that they had stopped one of the poachers from escaping.

Grandpa and Blackie came to where the girls had Kevin trapped.

"Thanks for catching that poacher," Grandpa said. "I can't run very fast with the arthritis in my legs. It sure was a good thing you girls were here or he would have gotten away."

The girls smiled. They were very proud of themselves.

*   *   *   *

After all the poachers were safely handcuffed into the bed of Agent Brown Bear's pickup, Denny and Randy proceeded to tell the girls what had happened after they had left the church.

They embellished some of the action, which made Brown Bear chuckle.

Then the girls told their story.

When the storytelling was complete, Grandpa and Brown Bear shook hands.

"It looks like you've got everything under control," Grandpa said. "I'll take these kids home so you can take those poachers into town and call their parents. Thanks for taking care of the boys. I don't know what we'll do with these two."

Brown Bear chuckled.

"Oh well, boys will be boys."

Then he looked at Denny and Randy and said, "Don't forget your horses; they are still tied up at the cabin."

"I almost forgot about the horses," Denny said. "It sure turned out to be an exciting night."

Everyone laughed.

*　　　*　　　*　　　*

Two days later, Sheriff Whippert's car drove into the yard after lunch.

Ty looked out the living room window and wailed, "What have we done wrong now?"

"If you've done nothing wrong, the sheriff won't punish you," Grandma assured him.

The Haskells went outside to greet the sheriff and Brown Bear. The agent opened the back door to let Blackie out.

"Look out!" Ty shouted as the dog got out of the car. "He's mean!"

"No, he's not," Denny objected. "He's a hero. He helped capture the poachers."

Brown Bear laughed.

"I brought Blackie over to meet you, Ty, so you can see what a nice dog he is."

Blackie stood quietly by Brown Bear's side as Ty came over to pet him. The dog wagged his tail and licked Ty's hand in a show of friendship.

Laddie, who was watching from the porch, came down to greet Blackie. The two dogs walked off to play, while the lawmen and the Haskells talked.

Laddie and Blackie walking

"We solved the case of the church vandalism too," Sheriff Whippert said proudly. "After your kids said they overheard the vandals talking about the damage they had done, we checked out the tire track we found behind the church the morning after the incident and compared it to the tires on Jay's pickup. They matched. When we confronted the teens with all our evidence, they confessed to all their crimes. Those boys have been doing a lot of no-good things this summer. They'll be punished, and their parents will pay some hefty fines."

Brown Bear complimented the children.

"Thanks to your fine detective work, we've solved the mystery of the deer shootings," he said.

The children beamed with joy.

Audrey spoke first.

"We were happy to help."

"Sure were," Ty said proudly.

"Thanks," the twins said together, trying to be modest. Then they both looked at Grandma and Grandpa.

"Maybe we don't have to be grounded anymore," Denny said hopefully.

"We'll see," Grandpa said. "The week's not over yet."

Brown Bear laughed. Then he shook hands with the children, called his dog, and got into the patrol car. The lawmen drove away while the Haskells waved good-bye.

CHAPTER 21

▼

A SAD FAREWELL

Where had the summer gone? It was the first weekend in August. The children's parents had called several days ago, when they had gotten back from Central America, to notify Abby and Josh that they would be down on Saturday to pick up the children.

Grandma felt a pang of sadness as she sat at the kitchen table preparing her menu for the weekend. She hoped the whole bunch would stay for the weekend and enjoy the lovely August weather.

"What are you doing?" Audrey asked Grandma as she entered the kitchen after completing her morning chores.

"I'm making a menu for the weekend, and then I'll bake some brownies. Want to help?"

"Cool," Audrey replied.

"We'll have to go to Aberdeen this afternoon to get some groceries. It will be the last weekend you kids are here, so we'll celebrate with a movie. Do you want to check the paper to see what's playing this afternoon?"

"Sure."

Audrey paused a moment and then asked, "Will Jenny and Denny be going along?"

Grandma laughed.

"Well, maybe it's time for a pardon. We'll talk it over at lunch today."

*   *   *   *

The children were busy eating their green beans smothered with homemade ranch dressing when Grandma said, "Josh, we'll need some groceries for the weekend. Maybe the children could go along and take in a movie while you and I shop."

"Well … I guess Jenny and Denny have learned their lesson. We'll all go today," Grandpa answered.

"Yay!" the children shouted at once.

Grandpa held his ears and shook his head slowly.

"Finish your lunch so we can get going. The movie starts at two."

*   *   *   *

Sylvia and Tom Thomsen, Ty and Audrey's parents, showed up first. They quickly got out of their car to grab the children, who were running from the house. Hugs and kisses were given in abundance all around.

After extensive greetings, Sylvia asked Audrey and Ty, "Have you been good this summer?"

Ty answered quickly, "We sure have!"

Audrey smiled shyly.

"Most of the time," she said.

Grandpa joined the conversation as he approached the group.

"They've been a lot of help around the farm," he said, choosing not to mention some of their misbehavior.

The children can tell their parents about that later—if they choose to do so, he thought.

"That's good to hear," Sylvia said. "What have you learned?"

"We gardened, fed the animals, milked Ulla, and mowed the grass," Ty answered with pride.

"That's wonderful!" Sylvia said, hugging her young son.

Then she turned to Audrey.

"What about you dear—what did you learn?"

"I learned to do some cooking and baking. I can fix delicious veggies, brown meat, and bake brownies," Audrey answered.

Her mother smiled.

"That's great," she said. "Now you can help with the cooking at home. Dad and I would love that."

"I'd love to help cook," Audrey said. "Maybe I could get a raise in allowance if I did more work around the house. I'll be in the eighth grade next fall. I'll need some neat new clothes, you know."

Her mom laughed.

"Yes, I know. I was an eighth-grader once, too, you know."

Audrey gave her mom a hug. She couldn't wait to get back to Sioux Falls to see her friends and go shopping at the mall.

✳   ✳   ✳   ✳

Mark and Heather Haskell, Jenny and Denny's parents, showed up about half an hour later.

The whole bunch of relatives was sitting on the porch visiting when they saw the car coming over the bridge. Denny and Jenny took off at a brisk run to meet their parents, who stopped the car halfway up the driveway to greet their children.

After a plethora of hugs and kisses, Mark asked the twins what they had done all summer on the farm.

"We worked," Jenny said, then added, "but it was fun. We—"

Denny interrupted. "We met these cool kids who live next door, and we learned to ride horses and—"

He stopped abruptly, not wanting to tell his parents that they had been grounded for the past three weeks.

"Oh?" his mother said. "And what happened then?"

Denny regained his composure.

"We'll tell you all about that later," he said. "Let's go talk to Grandma and Grandpa."

Denny grabbed his dad's hand and headed for the porch.

*   *   *   *

The children and parents couldn't stop talking. They had to tell each other about all the adventures they had this summer. The children were very careful not to mention the discipline measures Grandma and Grandpa had to take at times to keep them in line.

Grandma and Grandpa sat quietly beaming as they listened to their offspring talk. They were so proud of their children for successfully completing their mission to help people in Central America solve many of the eye-care problems that exist in developing countries. They were just as proud of their grandchildren for having learned responsibility, discipline, and some new family values this summer.

It's been a good summer, Grandma thought to herself. *Thank God everything worked out beautifully.*

It's been a fun summer, Grandpa thought, *but thank God they are all going home—I'm exhausted.*

＊　　　＊　　　＊　　　＊

On Sunday, after church and a wonderful dinner of chicken and dumplings, the children went to say good-bye to Cottontail, Hope, Ulla, Bessie—and even the despicable gander they had named Thor.

When they got to the clubhouse, Audrey suggested they do their club pledge and sign one more time before they left.

With their right fists held high, they repeated their club pledge: "I promise to follow the club rules and keep the club secrets, or I'll get kicked out by the other members."

When they brought their fists down over their hearts, a silent sadness fell on the group. They knew they would never see Cottontail again, because he was to be set free this fall. Ty hugged the rabbit tightly as tears welled up in his eyes.

"It's all right, Ty," Denny said, putting his arm around his young cousin. "Cottontail is almost grown up now, and he'll want to find some friends. He can't do that locked up in a cage."

"I know," Ty sniffled, "but I'm sad anyway."

By the time they were done saying good-bye to Hope, they were all crying. They took one another's hands as they left the clubhouse and said good-bye to Bessie and Ulla, who were drinking by the water tank. They waved good-bye to the goose family, who were sitting in the shade in back of the barn. The children didn't want to get too close to Thor—just in case he was in a foul mood. Then they walked slowly back to the house.

*   *   *   *

"I guess we're all packed and ready to go," Tom announced. "Get into the car, kids."

Little Ty started crying again as he said good-bye to Grandma and Grandpa.

Grandma hugged him.

"Why are you crying, sweetheart?" she asked.

"I like it here. I'll miss you and Grandpa and all the animals."

"We'll miss you too," Grandma and Grandpa said together as Grandpa picked Ty up to hold him one last time.

"Maybe you can come back next summer for another long stay," Grandma suggested.

"I'd love that!"

Ty's face broke into a big grin as the tears streamed down his cheeks.

Audrey spoke for the group.

"We'd all like to come back again next summer."

"Well then, it's all settled. We'll plan some more adventures next summer," Grandpa assured the children.

*   *   *   *

As the cars disappeared down the gravel road, Josh put his arm around his wife's shoulders.

"Well, Abby, do you suppose the kids will ever tell their parents what *really* went on around here this summer?"

Abby laughed.

"Not until they're all grown and gone from home."

"Maybe that's okay," Josh grinned. "It will be our secret, too."
"Cool!" Abby replied, giving her husband a high five.

Fawn drinking at the James river

978-0-595-42799-4
0-595-42799-5